VENGEFUL REIGN

THE MCNAMARA BROTHERS
BOOK 1

CARINA BLAKE

The Steele Press

ISBN: 978-1-954645-19-6

INTRODUCTION

Chicago's MacNamara brothers have a score to settle and revenge in their hearts as they lay waste to their enemies and claim the women that land in their arms.

When the youngest MacNamara disappears while in their father's care, war and vengeance stir in their veins, driving the brothers to hunt and destroy those involved. Finding their innocent little brother before it's too late was of the utmost priority. Jack MacNamara takes his position as the head of the family extremely seriously, including the love for his little brother. Leading the search for John sends the crime boss into uncharted territory and into the path of a petite teacher who needs to be taught a lesson or two when it comes to crossing the head of a crime family.

CHAPTER ONE

JACK

APRIL 2013

The meeting drones on longer than I'd like as the sun begins to settle over the Chicago skyline. The two men my attention is focused on sit in my office pretending to be respectable, concerned businessmen until it's time for the actual city officials to leave, but we all know they're anything but.

What started as an early morning conference turned into a four-hour meeting as they debated the merits of investing in a lakefront property.

"Very well, gentleman. At the moment, nothing further of value can be added to the discussion that will sway my opinion in either direction and I understand that you have a meeting with the mayor, correct?" I look over to the councilman to my left.

"Yes," he answers, checking his watch. He's been looking at it for over an hour, itching to leave, but fear has kept him glued to his seat. While the two men may intimidate the city council folk, they don't frighten me, so I don't mind ending this stalemate.

Finally, I was able to wrap it up, standing I addressed the men who had other pressing engagements with their constituents. "Thank you for joining me today. I'll go over your offer and make a decision later on this evening and have an answer over to your people by tomorrow."

"Thank you, Mr. MacNamara," Councilman Mason says, stuffing his papers into his briefcase while Councilman Ward does the same. My other guests look at their phones either addressing their own business matters or giving the nervous councilmen and their assistants a moment to pack up.

I walk the two councilmen and their assistants out toward the bank of elevators. Mason's assistant trips and I reach out, catching her. She looks up at me like I hung the world. "Be more careful," I growl. She straightens up and loses the needy girl look.

I fix my suit and clear my throat and address my assistant, Miss St. James. "Please serve more coffee in the conference room. I'll be in there momentarily." My assistant nods and does as I ask, pushing the cart inside with a hint of hesitation.

"Thank you again, gentlemen. It's been a pleasure." After shaking hands, I push the down button and wait for the elevator.

"Please think about our offer, Mr. MacNamara. It's a truly good deal, and we could truthfully use the investment," Councilman Ward says. That's the most honest thing that man has ever said to me, but I have to decide if I need the deal more.

"I will. I'll get back to you soon with my decision." The doors open, and they depart. My assistant is back at her desk, sorting mail, refusing to look up at me. She's been on edge since they walked in, and I can't say I blame her. As soon as they're gone, I check the weapon in my suit jacket before returning to my meeting with the two assholes in suits. Thugs masquerading as businessmen. Although, frankly I think the façade wore off hours ago.

Both Massimo Fieri and Ernesto Espinosa are menacing to the average person, drawing on their years of intimidation and brutality to get what they want and keep others at bay. I could give two shits what they think because I've dealt with a much more fucked-up man who was willing to let his wife suffer until she died just to have another son to neglect, so these pussies don't scare me.

The second I take a seat in my chair at the head of the table, Espinosa barks out, "MacNamara, have you considered the ramifications of going against the other families if you move forward with this deal on the waterfront?" My blood pressure rises higher than the fucking building were in. I could shoot this fucker right between the eyes for daring to challenge me.

My hand slams against the wooden table as I pop on my feet, sending my chair back and staring down at the other two families' heads. "Are you fucking threatening me?"

My actions might be violent, but my voice comes out cool and deadly calm.

The head of the Mexican Mafia shifts in his chair. "No, no. We're just saying," he stammers like a little bitch, and I want to pull out my gun and shove it in his mouth. Who the fuck does he think he is? I just saved his ass from embarrassment last month, and he comes in here with the idea that he can talk to me like that. I gave them a chance to change their minds, and this is what I get?

"I hear what the fuck you're saying, Ernesto. You're saying that we're of opposing opinions, and that my choices only work if they align with yours. If they don't, I'll regret it. Is that correct?"

"I'm just…" He's at a loss for words like a damn coward. I can see the weakness in his eyes and his slackness in his jaw.

"Either speak with your chest, or get out of my face. Next time, send a man to do business with me instead of a little bitch. I will do as I please. Until today, I hadn't been certain about the contract on the building on Lake Shore Drive, but now I believe the deal is a must. Now, both of you can excuse yourselves from my office, or I'll be forced to show my employees that you're not actually upstanding businessmen."

"Are they aware you're not either?" the other faux suit questions me. At least he has bigger balls, but I don't care for his challenge.

"They are aware that I'm not to be tested, Fieri. Are you?" The words exit my mouth through clenched teeth even though my voice doesn't raise a single decibel.

"Yes."

I stand up straight and tug on the edge of my suit, adjusting it calmly. "So, gentlemen, are we going to have a problem?"

"No. No, we won't," Fieri insists. The look in his eyes tells me that I'm dealing with a man of honor. Espinosa has never been one I could trust, but then again, they're both my rivals, so they can't really be trusted.

"Good. I would like us to move forward in this endeavor peacefully." I tip my chin, and they nod. Standing, each man grabs their things and then shakes my hand before exiting my conference room.

Fieri passes my assistant, Molly St. James, and gives her a lingering look, one that screams he'd like to pin her to the nearest surface and do unspeakable things to her. It's an intensity that unnerves her. I almost want to laugh and punch him at the same time, because she has a job to do and I don't have time for a flighty assistant.

My assistant comes into the room in their wake, holding her notepad against her chest like a shield. She's a petite blonde who has worked for the company for two years. I don't run my illegal operations here; however, there are times when they cross paths. "Mr. MacNamara, your brother called and asked that you call him immediately."

"Which brother?" My brow raises, and she takes a step back. The men that were here had definitely intimidated her. She was used to scum in suits, except these ones were deadly. The others just threw their money around and she just ignored their flirtations.

"Forgive me, sir," she stammers. Fixing her glasses, she bites her lip. "Ian, sir."

"Very well. I'll call him now. Make sure my guests exit the building."

"Yes, Mr. MacNamara." She shimmies back to her desk in a hurry. I almost feel bad that she's nervous, but that skittish behavior worries me. Can she be trusted? Is she just afraid of Fieri because he'd been looking at her like a meal, or is there more that she's apprehensive about? Employees understand my name is synonymous with danger, but that shouldn't make her skittish around me since I haven't given her a reason.

Instead of turning to my office, I slowly approach her desk without drawing attention to myself, and she nearly jumps out of her skin. "Sorry, Miss St. James, I didn't mean to startle you. May I ask why you seem so jumpy today?"

"Forgive me. It's just that I'm acquainted with the man that left." That doesn't sit well with me.

"Which one?" I ask, already knowing the answer after that brief exchange.

"Um...Massimo Fieri," she admits with a stammer, looking at her shoes.

"Why would he put you on edge?" She bites down on her bottom lip again, ready to gnaw it off. "Don't lie to me. Your job depends on the truth."

"Because she's been trying to deny our relationship. Right, Amore?" he says, stepping off the elevator.

I turn back to him and glare. "In my office now, Fieri."

He slides up to her side, cupping her elbow. "Molly, you try to run, and I won't let you get far." I watch as he makes his seductive threat, seeing my capable assistant try to fight the attraction that she obviously wants to deny.

He winks at her before following me into my office. The second the door is closed, I move to stand behind my desk. "You brought your woman in to spy on my company?" I questioned.

He chuckles, adjusting his cuffs. "Hardly. I only noticed her recently. My dealings with Molly have nothing to do with you or any of your matters. Rest assured, you'll be looking for a new assistant soon."

"She's not interested in you," I antagonize him.

"How long has it been for you? Molly is more than interested. She's just scared because she knows who I am and what I do." That's obvious.

I consider the complications and know what I have to do even if I don't like it. "Your relationship is a conflict of interest for me."

He shrugs. "That's easy. She quits. Excuse me." He smirks and walks out to the lobby and directly to Molly. I follow to the doorway of my office as he says, "Amore, grab your purse and coat."

"I'm not going with you," she huffs, crossing her arms.

"I'm afraid you are. You've just been fired. That night you spent with my dick stuffed between those pouty lips just cost you your job. Sorry." He doesn't sound the least bit sorry or conflicted about costing her job. In fact, his words and posture scream control and pride.

"You're not sorry, you bastard," she huffs, slapping his chest. I should say something, but there's nothing to do. She didn't deny their relationship, so she has to go. With a quick move, he tosses her over his shoulder.

"Put me down," she squeals. I watch from my office door as the scene unfolds. It's actually pretty entertaining despite the fact that it just cost me my assistant.

I'm grateful that the sound echoes from her desk because I don't miss an ounce of their discussion. "I will put your sweet ass down the second you agree to behave."

"I'll behave." He slides her down his shoulder, and they leave the building. I almost feel bad about losing her, but I can't have my rival's woman as my administrative assistant. There's just too much shit on the line. As much as I hate losing my damn assistant, I can't risk that shit.

As I slip back into my office, I remember that my brother called. I dial up Ian's number and wait for him to answer. "Jack, hey, are you in your office or at home?"

"At the office. Why?" I'm here most days, so I'm not sure why he'd ask, but then again, he wouldn't call me for no reason either.

"I got a strange feeling when I left the compound this morning. It's been bothering me, and I just landed in

Phoenix." The tension laced in his voice bothers me. It screams trouble, and I don't care for it.

My brows lift as I tilt back in my black leather chair, staring at the small picture frame on my desk. "What do you mean, a bad feeling?"

"It was too quiet."

"It's always quiet unless we're visiting John," I teased. Our youngest brother, who is only five, has been known to have massive tantrums. He's an adorable little guy with wavy brown hair and light brown eyes. Although you couldn't tell by looking at them because he'd never look you in the eye. It's one of the many quirks he has.

"I'll call over there shortly. Connor is in a meeting with my dealers at the docks this morning, so the compound should be low key." It's the way I preferred it. With my hands in so many pots, I didn't have time to borrow problems, so if the MacNamara estate remained peaceful, I was a happy fucker.

"I'm talking about the guards as well." A knot forms in my gut. "They weren't around no matter where I went except at the front gate."

My brother isn't prone to panic or concern, so the hairs on the back of my neck raise at his words. His fears become mine, even though I refuse to show it. It's my job to remain in control and tough, showing no signs of weakness.

"I promise that I'll look into your concerns, Brother."

"Thank you. I worry about John." We all worry about him, me more than anyone, but pulling him from my father's grasp was harder than it looked. I didn't have the time to rise a young boy who was mentally slow and required a lot of care.

I didn't even have time to find a wife. Fuck, maybe I should have taken the arranged marriage offer all those years ago. Then I would have had someone to watch John. He had a nanny, but that wasn't the same thing as a mother. He needed someone to love him as family and my wife would have to be someone who cared for John the way we all did.

"Have you seen him today?" I asked my little brother. All the details I could get on John's well-being was crucial to me.

He sighed before taking a moment to finally respond. "I said goodbye last night since I had to leave early this morning and I wasn't sure he'd be awake. Still, he was moody."

"Ha. What's new?" I chuckled. I wish things were different, but it doesn't stop us from loving John any less. Despite our little hiccups with our baby brother, he's a good boy with a sweet and gentle soul. Thinking anything could happen to him, sends my body into a frenzied panic.

As soon as I get off the phone with him, I call my father, checking in with him. "Jack, to what do I owe the pleasure of a call from you on a Monday morning?" he asks, sounding surprised, which I would expect because I wouldn't call him normally. "Are you checking on John?"

Is that my gut or just Ian's concern that sends doubt coursing through me. Why did he ask that?

"It's the afternoon and yes, I'm checking on John."

He scoffs his annoyance with me, but I'm used to it. Ever since he was forced to turn over the empire to me shortly after my mother died, he's been resentful. If he hadn't fucking lost his mind and let deals slip, killed random people, and nearly cost us millions of dollars he would still be the head of the family. "John's fine. He's getting changed for the day a little later than usual. He was throwing a fit after waking up in the middle of the night."

"So, you all just got a late start this morning?" I asked, wondering if we're just overreacting.

"Yes, Jack. What's up?" he sounds annoyed.

"Nothing. Just a bad feeling. Had a meeting with the councilmen over the LSD properties, and I'm about to sign the contracts."

"Tensions from the other families?" Gone is the annoyance and back is the former boss of the family. His interest is piqued and I sense some concern.

"Yes, but they'll deal with it. I've got to let you go."

"Okay, but let me know if there's anything I need to be worried about. I might not be the head of the family anymore, but that doesn't mean some don't see me as any less of a target."

"I know. I know." If he's a target then that makes my little brother a target, so I definitely need to reassure myself that everything at the house is safe. I ended the call, tapping my cell phone on my chin as I contemplated the possible safety precautions I could add to John's detail. He didn't leave the house, so it should be easier, but he also didn't like people near him, either.

I pull up my call log and dial Ian back. "Hey. I spoke with Dad, and there was nothing unusual at the house. They had a late morning because John didn't sleep well last night." Before I finish the last syllable, my phone goes wild with alarms for the estate. My blood runs cold.

"Hold up, Ian." Looking at my alert it reads: *Front Gate Damage.*

I turn on the home security cameras only to see them cut out.

"Son of a bitch. You were right. There's an attack on the grounds." I grab two things from my office and rush to the elevator, jabbing the fucker as fast as I can. "Gotta go. Need to call reinforcements," I say, ending the call with him because he can't help me from where he's at. He'll have to figure out shit later. All that matters is protecting the family that I can reach and destroying all those who dared to storm my home.

I'm rushing out of the building. My phone rang as soon as the metal doors opened. "Connor, someone's on the compound," I bark out. He must have gotten the alert as well.

"I'm on the way now. I got the alert. So far, I have six guys with me. Are you at the office?" Of course, he was on a job so he had a small team ready to pounce.

"Yes, I'm on my way out now. Damn it, Ian said something didn't seem right when he left this morning, but he couldn't explain it." He was right and now we're paying for it. I hope to hell our guys are handling it and when we get there all we got is some stupid fucks who learned a valuable lesson about crossing Jack MacNamara.

"Damn it. He messaged me too, but I blew him off." I try to remain calm and keep my head clear but all I can think of is John. We can't dwell on anything else at the moment.

"Whoever it is—is going to pay."

My security flies to my side as I reach the main lobby. "Boss, what is going on?"

"We need the vehicles, and I need all available at the estate. There's been an attack. I don't know the details, but John and my father are there." He pales beside me, knowing how much family means to us.

I call my father's phone, but it just continues to ring unanswered. "Son of a bitch." I hop into my armored SUV, and my driver with two of my men ride with me and we speed off into Chicago traffic. Damn it—our family compound is still forty minutes away at this time of day. There's no way to get there more quickly without a police escort, and that shit won't happen.

My phone rings as I get closer to the property. It's my father's phone. "Dad, what's going on?"

"It's Sam. We've been hit. Ten masked men came in with guns, rammed the front gate. Your father's unconscious." Sam's breathing heavy, labored.

"We're on our way now. Where is my brother?" I questioned him, hoping he was somewhere safe. I knew Sam was in danger and pain, but my brother was the most important being at the moment.

"I don't know. I'll find him." A shot rings out, and the line goes dead.

"Sam, Sam," I called out to the dead phone line. Fuck.

"Fuck, fuck, fucking hell. Speed up," I roar at my driver, as if he can control the assholes in front of us. I'm about to shoot these bastards if they don't open up a lane for me. A million and a half thoughts flood my mind and none of them are good which only makes my skin and muscles vibrate over my damn bones. I want to just jump out of my vehicle as if I could somehow get there faster. The expressway isn't as bad as it could be, but the ninety is crowded enough that we can't speed.

As we approach the manor, a new sense of dread fills me. The line of trees that lead to the property is ablaze. I called the police department, and they've already been alerted that there has been an incident. Thank goodness, because all that matters is my little brother.

Frankly, I don't give two fucks what happens to my father. After all that he's done, he can rot in the ground where he lays, but my brother is everything to me. There was no way in hell I'd stop until I had him safely in my arms.

CHAPTER TWO

JACK

WHEN I ARRIVE, THERE ARE MEDICS AND POLICE along with fire trucks blaring toward the blazing trees.

The houses aren't burning, but my front gate is smoldering. The wind sends embers past my vehicle as we drive and I wonder if the fires will spread with the crisp air day. The massive compound holds four mansions: one for each of us, and several smaller homes for some of our staff members. The grounds are extensive, but the security is tight. Well, so I thought it motherfucking was until an hour ago.

The cops are at the front, stopping the vehicles. I jump out and immediately present my ID. "Whoa, whoa. No entry yet."

"I'm the fucking owner of this entire estate. Where are my father and brother?" I roar, wanting answers before I bust their heads open. I knew it wouldn't do me any good because there were too many of these assholes around and I wasn't in my right mind.

"You father and brother?" the jagoff in uniform asks like it's a difficult question. He has my motherfucking name and therefore I'm looking for the other MacNamaras.

"Yes, Jack and John MacNamara."

"Jack has been taken to the hospital in serious condition with a gunshot wound and several injuries, and we haven't located John. How old is John?" I can feel the blood leach from my face, but I hold it together because maybe they're hiding.

"He's five. He should be with his nanny. Her name is Joanne. She's a short woman in her forties or fifties." I don't fucking know, but now I'm pissed that I don't have the answers.

"There's no female on the premises that we've encountered so far." What the fuck? Did she get John to safety? Where are they?

I look around and see several dead bodies covered by tarps. Rushing past the police, I lift up the first one and find the remains of my guards in pieces. It must have been from the explosion. One by one, I look for them. My chest burns with rage. There are so many buildings to search, but I don't want the police on my property.

I turn around and around, unsure what the fuck I'm doing. Getting control of my emotions, the same cop is next to me again, pressing his hand on my shoulder. "Do you need a medic, sir?"

"No, I'm okay. I need to find my little brother," I muttered. Now wasn't the time to free the fuck out. I had to remain in control and keep a level head.

"We'll continue looking," he insists.

"I'll pull up the surveillance footage and see if they can be found." The only house that seems to have been attacked is my father's. His is the closest to the entrance. Had this been deliberate, or was it because of the distance to the entrance?

"Maybe they fled because they didn't make it that far," a man in a suit with a police badge says, answering my unspoken question. My brows kick up, wondering about the cops. I obviously didn't have a good relationship with them and they wouldn't want to assist when it came to finding my little brother.

"Jack," Connor shouts from the entrance where more cops are blocking his way in.

"Connor, come here. John's missing," I snarl, wanting to tear this place apart. He runs toward me, pushing past the assholes.

"What the fuck are they doing here if they aren't finding our brother? Fucking useless fucks," he snaps, glaring at the cops.

"We just arrived. We need permission to search the premises," the professional dick said.

"You can search the grounds, but we'll check the house. Our security shows they didn't get farther than the main house here," Connor says.

"Mr. MacNamara, it wouldn't be wise to hinder our investigation when it comes to your brother's location."

"Do you know something, Detective?" I snarl, getting in his face. My body dwarfed his and he can't stop his own reaction as he backs up a step.

"No, but you aren't being fully cooperative," he says with brass balls.

"I just had my home invaded. Forgive me if I don't trust anyone to look for my brother. *Anyone.* We will look for him. You can look for him outside of our estate. Clean up this mess, and we'll check out the surveillance to the gate that was demolished on my damn property."

"Don't scrub the footage." He was testing my patience. I wouldn't erase a damn thing because it all pointed to where my brother would be and that's more important than anything else.

"I won't." I want these assholes off my property now. The first thing I need to do is go into my father's house and look for John. "Connor. We need to search the old man's home first. According to the logs, it's the only one where the sensors were accessed. The rest of the homes have been locked down." When there is a break-in, the houses go into full lockdown unless we use special exits.

Our men used them, but I fucking see them lying dead on the ground. Whoever these pricks were, they waited until we had the least amount of security on the estate and the least of us here. This was a setup and a half, but to what motherfucking end?

We search the entirety of my father's mansion with all of our men, and not a trace of our brother is found and it looks like they ransacked the place and left. "Where is John?" I mutter to myself.

Just as I exit his front door, my phone rings and the caller ID is Rush Medical Center. "Mr. MacNamara?"

"Yes, this is him." I didn't have time unless she had information on my brother. Did the nanny take him to the hospital?

"I'm nurse Hernandez. I'm calling about your father." This isn't a priority to me.

"Is my father dead?" I asked, wondering if he didn't survive his injuries.

"No, we're calling to let you know your father is out of surgery."

"Thank you. What were the extent of his injuries?"

"A bullet wound to his arm and one to his calf. Several bruised ribs and a black eye." So they wanted to inflict pain, but they didn't kill him like they did everyone else here. Why?

"When will he be released?" I asked with obvious impatience.

"We can release him tomorrow."

"Thank you. Don't release him until I arrive personally to pick him up. Understand?" I informed the woman on the phone.

"Yes, sir."

"Good." I end the call and then find the fucking detective up my ass. "Excuse the fuck out of you. Are you here to fuck me, or is there a reason you're breathing down my neck?"

"Who were you talking to?"

I glare at this fucking detective who never even gave me his name. He came strolling up to me with audacity and I'm not in the mood for his shit. "None of your damn business. Are you done here? I need everyone off my property already."

"You don't tell me what you need done. This is a major crime scene, Mr. MacNamara. It seems you don't give a shit what happens to your little brother. Did you have something to do with his kidn…" He can't get the words out because my hand is around his throat, cutting off his air supply as I lift him off the ground.

"Jack, drop him. Fuck, he's a cop." My brother's right, but it doesn't matter at the moment. This cunt has a problem with me and I have one with him.

"I don't give a fuck. He's trespassing. He's a piece of shit who's probably working with the kidnappers, and he dared to insult me." I glare at the fuck. "Getting hard to breathe?" The other cops don't move in even though they reach for their guns, but my men all have their hands on their weapons as well. I'll have everyone laid out in seconds.

"Do try something, and this place will be a round motherfucking two bloodbath. Don't come back on my fucking property again, you useless piece of shit in a cheap suit," I snarl, dropping the fuck on the ground. "I'll find my brother myself, and if I find out that any cops helped in getting my brother kidnapped, I'll make sure there will be hell to pay."

I turn to Johnny B. "Get these assholes off my land. I have to find my brother." There was a lot to discuss, and I couldn't do it with cops around being nosy. I had an idea of who was involved, but it wasn't the time or the place to have that conversation. "Connor, we need to speak in private." He nods and follows me alone.

CHAPTER THREE

JACK

I STORMED INTO MY PALATIAL HOME AFTER checking that my security was still intact, going straight to the bar in my office to pour a glass of whiskey. My brother follows suit, and we drink them down while my mind whirls with questions. Who the fuck would do this?

"We need a better look at the cameras." I know they attacked all the entryway ones so they could operate unseen, but they didn't go for the ones that extend toward the path toward my house. Connor's house is next, down the road from my father's, so they didn't go that far down. They took my father's house, cutting every signal in the way.

I hit the enter key on the computer, waiting for the fucker to wake up, and then I enter my code. Once I'm in, I slide down the panel to the large ninety-inch flat screen that is equipped to display ten 4k-quality split screens at any given time. My alarm went off at 1:22 in the afternoon, so I loaded the time code to 1:20 and focused on the exterior. My brother and I are the only ones I trust enough to view this.

As we take a seat in front of the large screen, I hit play and allow everything to unfold. We both do our best to hold it together as we watch our comrades explode in front of our eyes. The guards at the front gate go flying. They were completely unaware of the explosion headed their way. Both men were taken by surprise, and it guts me.

"Fuck," Connor snarls, slamming his whiskey glass down.

"Pay attention." Three large white vans speed through the gates, riding over the mangled, burned remains. As they do, several of my men run from their locations with guns ready, armed for war, but they were unprepared and the guys in the white van jumped out with full-autos, unloading them. Three more of my men fall. One of the vans rides straight past the chaos and to my father's door just as the cameras go off.

"Switch it to the one from my driveway," Connor demands, slapping my shoulder anxiously.

"I know what the fuck I'm doing," I bark out, shaking my head at him. Double checking the time stamp, I switch to camera number five, and I get a different angle. It shows the van pulling up to our father's home and five armed men covered from head to toe storming the residence. Moments later, my father and my brother are sneaking out a back entrance with the nanny, trying to go around and head toward the other houses, but they're spotted.

My father is shot, and the nanny fights them, but there isn't much effort in it. My little brother is gagged while he continues to fight them before he goes limp. We spot the cloth over his mouth and know they drugged his little ass. Son of a bitch.

"Those bastards." My father gets up and attempts to fight, but they kick him twice before popping him on the shin and then driving off with the nanny and my little brother. I crush the glass in my hand.

"Son of a bitch—what are you doing? There's enough blood loss around here." We both move quickly to the kitchen to clean up the damn blood, but honestly, I don't give a shit because I need to figure out who these assholes are and why they took my brother after killing half my guards and leaving my father to bleed out on the damn front steps of his home.

"Do you think they'll be calling us for a ransom?" Connor questions as I rinse off the blood in my kitchen sink. The shit isn't too bad. I have a small cut from a shard that dug into my palm.

"Boss, is everything okay?" He looks down and sees the blood pouring through my fingers into the sink.

"Yes, Johnny. I got a little pissed. Get the medical kit from the bathroom." He nods and leaves.

"They have to want something from us. There's no other damn reason to have stolen John." My head spins from the rage. I want to crush a motherfucker's head now. I don't even feel the damn pain in my hand I'm so fucking angry.

"Could you stop fucking clenching your fist? I'm trying to clean this shit up." He wraps a kitchen towel around my hand, but I'm not concerned about anything other than my vengeance. It's already consuming me, filling me up, darkening my already cold heart.

"Sorry. I want to kill someone."

"And you will. Do you think it has to do with the deal this afternoon?" Johnny comes back through the kitchen door with the kit.

"Johnny, do you know all the men we lost today? I only saw about six men. We need to notify all of their families," I say, wanting to give him something to do while I keep our discussion private.

"Yes, Boss. I've already started making a list, and Mickey went in the ambulance with Mr. MacNamara."

"Is there anyone else at the hospital?"

"No, just the cops," Johnny says.

"Send one of my father's men to look over him, or better yet, after you get a list together, I'd like you to watch over him. I can't trust anyone at the moment. Especially anyone that might work for him."

"Yes, Boss." He nods and disappears from the kitchen, leaving Connor and me alone again.

I continued our previous conversation and answered his question. "No, the attack was happening while I was working on the deal. I hadn't even signed the contracts, but I'm not putting it past those assholes."

"I'm glad Johnny is going over to monitor Dad. We need to have someone watching his ass." I roll my fucking eyes and scoff as he tapes up my hand after applying some butterfly stitches.

"Personally, I don't give a fuck, but if he has information, I don't want anyone finishing the job they started," I stated. My father was a piece of shit.

"I don't think they wanted to kill him. If they did, he would have been shot in the head."

"True, like they did Sammy. Either way, I want answers, and I want these fucks dead and my little brother back," I snarl, slamming my good hand on the cold countertop.

"'Our' little brother, and we will, Jack. We will," he says, pressing his hand to my shoulder. "Now let's get back to your office so we can see anything else we missed before you lost your shit."

"I was just the one to do it first. Don't tell me my other glass isn't fucking cracked."

"Well, I sure as fuck wouldn't trust pouring that high-quality liquor in it right now." He chuckles, shaking his head and walking back to my office. I follow, feeling heavy hearted. My little brother must be frightened as fuck right now. John isn't your typical five-year-old, and it scares me even more because they could kill him because of it.

John was born with brain damage, according to my father. My mother had a traumatic delivery, and she never recovered. He never mentally developed properly and was prone to fits of hysterics. The risk of his kidnappers killing him because of it was more than likely. Every minute he is in their hands is a minute too long. I'm grateful he has his nanny with him. She is one of the few who can at least calm him down. The only one who can get through sometimes.

Connor and I watch the video again, focusing on the vans, and each one is unmarked and indistinguishable. It's the movement toward the van that catches my interest and then my brother's. "Is she helping them?"

"No, she wouldn't," I mutter. She cares for my little brother and wouldn't harm him.

"Maybe she's only cooperating enough to stay alive," Connor adds. It makes sense because there are bodies strewn about, and if Joanne wants to protect John, she'll need to stay alive.

"We need to find them, and soon," I respond, focusing on the now paused screen, staring at the final images of my little brother before he's tossed into a van. "We'll find you, buddy, and we'll destroy all those who took you."

"I need to call in some favors with the traffic cops." I made calls to several people to get the footage which should be sent to me in the next few hours.

"What's next?" Connor asks, getting off his call with the police who wanted more information. They knew better than to call my ass.

"Anything from those assholes?"

"Nothing of importance," he grunts. "More inane questions that aren't going to find John any faster." I nodded, thinking about my next moves.

Suddenly the door to my office swings open, and my gun is trained on the bastard. "Fucking hell, Ian," Connor roars at our younger brother, who looks like shit. His floppy black hair is a mess and his eyes are bloodshot.

"I got here as fast as a plane can go." He's saying so much with so little, which scares me when it comes to Ian. The motherfucker is a different level of crazy. Connor and I kill people with pleasure and straightforward necessity. Ian will look for creative methods before finding something fun to do right after. One time, he offed eight people before going to a carnival, winning John eight stuffed animals—one for each of the people he killed.

"Did you fly one yourself?" Connor asks, staring at my wild-eyed brother.

"Yes."

I cock my brow, wondering if he stole the motherfucker or if he borrowed it because our private jet has a pilot and as far as I'm aware is still in the hangar at O'Hare.

"Don't tell me you stole one," I challenge.

"No, I borrowed a friend's. Now what the fuck is going on?" We give my brother the details as he polishes off three glasses of my whiskey like it's water.

"Could you at least savor it?" Connor complains, glaring at our younger brother.

"Fuck off. We need to find him. This is all my fault. There's no way I should have left this morning. I felt like something was wrong." I understand the anger and shame he has. He called us sounding worried this morning and it was well deserved. Still, he was better off far away.

"And you might be dead or in the hospital. It was a straight-up ambush, bodies lying everywhere. We lost a total of ten men, Dad is in the hospital, and John and Joanne have been nabbed," Connor says, gripping his shoulder.

"I would have killed anyone who dared come for him."

"I know. We all know, but we don't know who they are or what they're capable of, Bro. We need to figure out how they knew where to look and how they knew we wouldn't be home. This was strategic. They came for John, and John alone. As soon as they had him, they were gone as if nothing else mattered."

He swallows hard, running his hand through his shaggy black hair. "What's your plan, Boss?"

"I already put in for our contacts to pull all the traffic cameras leading away from our property. Until that happens, we need to do everything we can to look for a lead."

"Where the fuck do we begin?" Connor growls, rubbing his hand over his face.

"I want every call made to the gates and to Dad, and Joanne's phone checked too. Someone knew they would be here. We need to comb over the area, and I need someone to back-hack into our system and see how they were able to cut the feed to the cameras in front." Each runs on a different line intentionally to prevent a massive system failure and hacking, which means they knew how to get into it and knock out the right cameras.

"Damn, which means they are sophisticated enough to hit us hard. They have to be a big operation, or just crazy as fuck," Ian says.

"They're dead either way. I want answers, our brother John back, and then a bunch of dead bodies littering our path on the way home." I'm on a motherfucking warpath and I want the world to know it. My brothers nod in agreement before we part ways, working on answers, getting the men to do their job.

The first thing I need Connor to do is contact a contractor to rebuild the gate and have it reinforced. An impenetrable steel frame will be a must so that an explosion won't work. Fucking pricks got lucky that we were woefully unprepared for the level of brass balls on the bastards to play that dirty, but we've learned our lesson and that won't happen again.

This place isn't just a compound of wealth and opulence. It was now going to become a fortress—Fort Motherfucking MacNamara—and I was now General Jack, holding this bitch down.

CHAPTER FOUR

JACK

IT IS TWO IN THE MORNING WHEN MY EYES finally get the better of me and begin to grow heavy. My sleep doesn't last long because my phone blares, waking me up at four with Johnny on the line, informing me that the contractors are on their way here. Damn—I guess when you threaten a motherfucker, shit gets done fast. "I'll be ready to meet with them in thirty minutes."

I'm quickly showered, dressed, and shaved, running on almost no sleep, but now isn't the time to slow down. My family is suffering, and everything we built is hanging in the balance. More importantly, my little brother is missing.

"Mr. MacNamara, I was informed that you need this project done yesterday, so my team can work on it, but it will still take two weeks. What your man said you're asking for requires measurements, modifications, and intricate coding."

He looks nervous, as if what he said is going to get him shot where he stands, but as a businessman, I understand there are only so many things you can do with labor, and curing metal with other hardening agents to a stone wall takes time. It can't just be done in a day. Not to mention all the wiring that goes into opening the sliding gates. The project won't be small.

"I understand. Make it happen in that time, and you'll be paid double." What I want is insane on such short notice and should take months of planning, but that's why I have the best come all the way out here for it.

"Yes, sir." He nods vigorously with a smile. "We'll get to work right now." He turns and goes straight to his work truck where I can see a younger version of himself sitting in the passenger seat. A son—someone to follow in his footsteps. I'm thirty-six, and I haven't considered that in my life. A family, someone to leave all of this to when I'm gone. Hell, none of us have considered that part of our lives yet and we're not getting any younger, but now isn't even the time to contemplate a life like that.

"Boss, do you need some coffee or something?" Johnny asks. The growing concern in his voice would normally set me off because there isn't room for weakness in my position, but this is John we're talking about. Everyone knows that he is important to me.

"Thanks, but I'm going to grab some shortly, Johnny. Let's go inside and make a game plan before I head to the hospital to pick up my father."

Connor comes into my office an hour after I sent Johnny on a mission. It's only eight in the morning. "Damn, did you even sleep?"

"Two damn hours," I grumble, tossing back the rest of my coffee in a large gulp because I have no time to waste and I need a serious pickup.

My phone goes off. "It's the hospital." I put the phone on speaker and hold it out so we can both hear the person on the other end.

"May I speak with Jack MacNamara, Jr.?" a woman asks with a tense formality that reeks of professionalism and annoyance.

"Jack MacNamara speaking."

"Hello, I'm Nurse Flanagan. I'm calling about your father."

"Is he dead?" A man can only hope.

"No, no. He's improving quite rapidly. Although I must inform you that he has become belligerent and wishes to be released now."

"I apologize for his behavior and will try to get him under control."

"We understand the circumstances, given his son's disappearance. However, if he doesn't behave, we will have to sedate him." It would be hilarious if I wasn't already wanting to shoot someone in the head.

"We understand. Please don't do that. Inform him that I will be there shortly to pick him up," I say. I fucking need answers, and he's the best person to give them right now. I want John back like yesterday even if I have to deal with my father's bullshit.

"Thank you, sir." I end the call, and we both run out of my office toward the front door.

WHEN WE ENTER MY FATHER'S ROOM, THE asshole has the nerve to cop an attitude like the ungrateful bastard he is. "Took you long enough to get here. We need to get out of this place and find him now. Where have you been?" my father asks me, his face all fucked up. He's holding his side, and I'm glad about it. Giddy, in fact. He deserves the pain he gets for letting this happen to my brother. It's his job to protect my brother at all costs, and he fucking failed.

"Where the fuck was I?" I question, snarling and leaning in as Connor presses a hand to my chest to hold me back. "Why didn't you shoot the bastards before they got a hold of him? Why didn't you toss John in one of the safe rooms before it was too late?"

"I was on the bloody fucking ground, bleeding and broken."

My nose flared as I challenge him. He still fucking thinks he's in charge, but he lost that battle a long time ago when we were nearly killed because of him. "You should be dead, apparently, like our other men are. They let you off lightly, it would seem."

"Ha! How else do you think they're going to get the money out of me?" he asks like he's so damn smart, but I'm one minute from sticking my fingers in his wounds and watching him bleed out.

"I suppose he has a point there," Connor says. Barely, because there's me they have to bargain with.

"Do you have any idea who they are?" I question, demanding answers as we stand in front of the nurses' station.

"So, do you think we can have this conversation somewhere else?" my brother asks, raising his brows while turning his head left and right, pointing out all the attention we're drawing.

I look at all the nosy-ass women, and they turn their heads when they catch my expression that says *mind your fucking business*. "Let's get out of here," I snarl, grabbing the old man's arm.

"Excuse me. I need you to sign these before he can leave," a nurse skittishly says, holding a clipboard out toward me. I take the papers from her shaky hands and look them over quickly, their standard release forms informing me that if something should happen to him after he leaves the hospital, they're not liable for it. I don't give a fuck, anyway. This man has pushed me to my limits over the past few years since my mother's death and even before, so I quickly sign off and tell them to bill me.

We walked out of the hospital and straight to my vehicle. My brother helps my father inside, and I go straight to the driver's side because hell if I'm going to give him a hand. So far he's being a prick and less than helpful. As of this moment, he's essentially useless.

Tension between us has grown over the years, especially when it comes to John and his welfare. He may be his father, but he's been anything but a good one and has always pushed me away from my little brother. Since I wanted him to see other specialists outside of my father's private doctors. If I wasn't running the family business, I would have snatched him up and forced my father's hand. Once we get him back, that's exactly what I'll do, whether he likes it or not.

"I need to know everything that happened before I go another inch farther," I say, pulling over onto the side of the road just a few minutes into the drive.

"I know you don't believe me, Son, but I love him. Maybe not as much as I should as a father, and not as much as your mother would have loved him, but I do. I want him back, and I'm going to hurt everybody who took him from us." I hear the words coming out of his mouth, but I don't give them any credence. They are meaningless in my mind because I've seen them together and there is no way he gives two shits about John.

I slam my fist into the steering wheel. "Just tell me what the fuck happened so we can find him and find those sons of bitches." Connor stares at me like he's watching a wild animal about to attack and he's not sure if he should try to calm me down or let me loose. Frankly, I might lose it with the old man if he doesn't give me something right now.

"We'll find him. I won't rest until I do."

I put my vehicle back in gear, hit the road, and drove toward the house. "Did you get a good look at the bastards?"

He shakes his head. "No. They were masked, and I was shot quickly." Of course, proving to be useless. If he was anyone else, he'd have a bullet in his head already.

"So, they grabbed Joanne?"

He shakes his head. "I don't know. At first, it sounded like they did because she was screaming, but then I heard her running and asking for help, and then gunfire started going off." We saw her in the van, but that doesn't mean she didn't escape. Then again the old man was probably ducking to save his own ass.

"This is going to be harder than we thought. We can't involve the police any more than they already have been. The fucking governor is on our ass already," Connor adds, grumbling to himself. I'm sure there are some illegal warrants being thrown around, but we're extra careful.

"You're damn right about that, but do you think that asshole could be involved?" my father asks.

"That son of a bitch could be," my brother says.

Connor's phone goes off and he answers it, snarling, "Tell me you have something and not wasting my time." He nods and then mutters, "Get it to me, and if you find anything else, don't hesitate to give me a call. We want everything you got on the van, including reflections. Follow the cameras as far as you can." He ends the call and then says, "They got the video of a white van leaving the area in a hurry. They're trying to follow it, but it's rush hour and there are dozens of white vans passing until they reach the expressway."

Shit. This is exactly why they did it. Of course they wanted to blend in, and hell, there could be more than just the several white vans involved for all we know. They might have transferred John to another vehicle before we realized it.

CHAPTER FIVE

NORA

MAY 2013

"Thanks for tonight," I say, even though I don't mean a single word. Dinner with Jeremy had been awful. We've hit a major bump in the road, and this relationship is over. Three months of going back and forth, and yet getting nowhere. He's outgrown his welcome in my life and I'd like to move on from him, but I need to do it delicately. There's something about him that gives me a sense that he won't take the breakup well.

"Don't you want to invite me in?" he asks, winking with a casual smirk. I used to think it was cute, but now it's just annoying. There's something about the way he stares that gives me an uncomfortable feeling. All evening, he's been hinting at sex—the one thing I've been putting off.

"Actually, I'm kind of tired, and I have to work in the morning." I shouldn't have gone out on a Thursday night, but that's the only time he was available.

"Are you serious, Nora? You're doing this again?" He whines like a child.

"I have no idea what you're talking about," I insist, wanting to distance myself from him, but we're in his tiny sports car and there's no room.

"Bullshit. You're pushing me away. All damn dinner I noticed it. I have to work a lot, and I can't help it, baby. I miss you, and instead of working on it, you want to shove me away."

"Look. I'm not in the mood." We've gotten close to doing the deed, but I can't bring myself to want to sleep with him. When he touches me I get too uncomfortable, like it's just not right.

"Are you fucking someone else?" he barks, glaring at me with eyes that suddenly have darkened, almost menacingly.

"No, of course not." I had a feeling he'd go there. Isn't that the usual standby the second you don't want to put out?

"Prove it." Wow, that's a bit excessive. A chill runs down my spine and then I stiffen up that motherfucker. How dare he. I'm not the one claiming to work overtime or out with the guys.

"Are *you* sleeping with someone else?" I toss back his way.

He throws his head back like I slapped him. "Oh, I see what you're doing. You're trying to turn this around to get out of shit."

"No, because the person who makes baseless accusations is usually the one having the affair." It's a warm night, but he has the windows rolled up. I need them down because it's too damn hot and I feel like I can't breathe because it's so overwhelmingly tense in here.

His expression softens, and he takes my hand. I try to pull it free, but he holds it tight. "My sweet Nora, I'm not cheating on you. I just want to see you more."

"So why are you always working late?" I ask, testing that sudden calm. He's always working odd hours.

"To make money. It's not like I'm rolling in dough." He keeps his voice calm, but his tone hardens. Something about it just feels like a lie.

"Look, I'm going to bed. I have to work in the morning, and I need to think about things." I quickly pull my hand from his, yank the handle, and get out of his car. Turning around before closing the door, I give him a sweet smile and say, "Goodnight, Jeremy."

I catch an evil sneer crossing his face before he twists his expression into a soft, gentle, forgiving smile. "We'll talk tomorrow, Nora. Get some sleep."

I walk into the house without looking back. The dang jerk didn't even bother to wait until I got inside before driving away. He must be pissed at me for not putting out. What a gentleman. I'm not having this argument with him, and I wouldn't have even mentioned it tonight. We've both said enough, and I don't want to make things worse. All I want to do is get out of these heels, undo this bra, and fall face first on my bed.

I unlock my door, step inside, and kick off my heels with a deep sigh. Sometimes it's so nice to have this house for myself. Right before I turned eighteen, I left home and moved East, buying this home with my inheritance from my grandparents. Money gifted to me just in the nick of time.

My beautiful little house makes me happy and peaceful. I can't wait for the weekend to come and relax with a book. Smiling, I strip down and collapse on my bed, grateful that I don't have to deal with any problems as a twenty-three-year-old. Tomorrow I'll go into work, play with the kiddos, and give them all the love and attention I can before ending my relationship with Jeremy.

But for now, I'm just going to sleep.

MY PHONE HAS BEEN GOING OFF LIKE CRAZY with an unknown number. No voicemails left, either; like that's going to make me answer. It reeks of my parents or my brother. Nope, not taking their calls. Not a chance in hell. We're not on speaking terms, and it's the whole reason I changed my last name and moved far away from them.

By lunchtime, I've turned the damn thing off. It isn't like I have anyone I want to talk to anyway. The situation with

Jeremy can be dealt with over the weekend when I don't have to wake up early the next day and I don't have to deal with a bunch of small children and anxious mothers.

"Nora, dear. There's a woman to see you," Sarah says, stepping into the playroom as quietly as possible, attempting not to disturb the kids at play. I'm a paraprofessional at an elementary school. We have several special education, or SPED, teachers, however, each child needs love and care, so we could always use more. Unfortunately, our hands are tied behind our backs because funding is an issue. I love these little ones.

"Can you take over for me?" I had a play circle with three of the pre-school kiddos. They love Sarah, so it shouldn't be a big deal.

"Sure. She's in the main office." I stand up and leave the room after giving the kids each a brief hug and a promise to return. One grows anxious and the other two couldn't care less that I left.

When I walk into the office, I see someone who shocks me to my core. Someone I haven't seen in almost six years. Not since I moved out of Chicago. An icy chill shoots up my spine, and my trepidation about my parents' calls flood my mind. What does she have to say? Please tell me it's not terrible news. As much as I hate my parents' choices, I'm not sure I'm prepared to hear of their deaths.

My mouth drops open in shock, and I wonder what she could possibly say. "Julia, what are you doing here?" I ask, voice quaking.

"I know it's been a long time. I didn't think you'd recognize me," she says with a half-hearted smile. She's aged a lot more than before, but how could I've forgotten her. It's only been over half a decade since we've seen each other.

She's always been kind to me. She's the one who helped me run away all those years ago, even giving me access to my inheritance so I didn't have to live on the streets. I thought I would have to leave that money behind. I'm not sure how she worked her magic, but the lawyer transferred the money while not letting my family know where I ran off to.

Whatever the reason she's here, I owe the past five and a half plus years of freedom to her. I throw my arms around her, and she hugs me. "It's so good to see you again. I can't believe you're here. What brings you to Philadelphia?" Then, I hear whimpering that turns into a whine. "Who do you have with you?"

"Can we speak in private?" she whispers, looking around the small administrative office as if someone's watching.

"Yes. Come in here." I lead her over to a conference room where she brings the little boy, who is skittish and doesn't make eye contact. He's too young and doesn't look like her, so I doubt he's her son, but he could be a relative.

"Please sit." She sets him down at the table and takes a set of tactile toys from her large tote bag and places them on the table in front of him. He takes them and throws them across the room. We both gently and quietly pick them up and set them down, pretending not to notice his behavior, and sit back in our chairs.

"Julia, why are you here?" I ask, biting on the edge of my lip as I wait for an answer.

"The thing is...I need you to take him in," she finally answers, stealing a glance at the little boy.

I suppose she must have learned from my family that I'm a teacher. Despite the name change and no contact, I learned that my brother found me and kept his distance. "Okay. Does he have his paperwork? I didn't know you moved into the area."

"It's not like that, Nora." A tear rolls down her cheek. I reach to the middle of the table and hand her a box of tissues. She takes two tissues, balling them up in her hand. "Thank you."

"What do you mean?" I ask, setting the box on the table.

She wipes away the tears and clears her throat. "It's a lot more complicated than that. I know that it's asking a lot, and that we haven't spoken to each other in a long time, but this is very important. You're the only person I could turn to when it comes to John and his safety."

She pauses and looks at the little boy who is struggling with the gadget, banging it on the edge of the table. She places her hand over his calmly. He shoves it away and continues without a word. "I need you to take him in as one of your students and also as your ward."

My ears ring as the blood rushes to them. Did she just ask me to raise him? "What do you mean? Who is he to you?"

With a huge sigh, she answers, "He is my godson. Unfortunately, I can't say too much more, or I'll be risking your safety and everyone you know. Please. It's very important that he gets the love and help he needs. It will only be temporary. His parents are dead, and his extended family is out to have him eliminated."

My mouth falls open as my own set of tears fall from my eyes. "Oh, my goodness." I look at the little boy wondering so many things. When I glance back at Julia, she's staring at him. "Why haven't you gone to the police with this?" I asked.

"Nora, his family is well connected. I don't have to tell you how that goes." She had to remind me of family, and there it is—the reason she came to me. The one person who owes her more than anyone else. A favor for a favor. A life for a life. She's right, though. As much as I don't like this, and as uncomfortable as I feel, maybe I am the only one who can help them.

"You're right, Julia. Is that where he got the scar?" He has a scar on his left cheek that looks vicious and yet fading. I can't believe someone would hurt him so terribly.

"Yes. It's still healing, but yes, that's where he got the scar. It's been crazy on the run, but I need him cared for properly and I know you can help him. He was born with a disability and you're a special needs teacher, so it's perfect. I want him to have the life, the long life he deserves."

My chest aches as I consider what she's saying. "I'll do all I can. I promise, but we still have to fill out all the necessary paperwork."

"Don't worry about all of that. I have a friend helping me, and by the end of the day, you'll have everything you need. Just trust me." She stands up, walks around the conference table, and gives me a big hug. "John, I have to go."

"You're not taking him with?" I figured she'd give me a little time before leaving me with him. After all, he's not even a student or anything.

"Well, let's just say that I have some things to do, but you'll see me after school."

"School ends at four," I tell her. She gives me a smile and a nod.

"His car seat will be waiting." She walks out of the conference room without a backward glance.

I stare at the little boy who doesn't make any eye contact, and I wonder if he's seen any specialists for his autism yet. She didn't name his disability, but it's quite clear from a professional standpoint that he's autistic. I watch him for a few more minutes as he seems unaware that she left. Strange. Then I see he's fascinated with the toy car. I put away my work things and check on him again, but he hasn't budged with his car. "Ja," he mutters. "Ja, Ja," he repeats more excitedly this time, driving his car, speeding the car around before he hugs it. He still hasn't realized that she left yet, but he must be calling for her. That's what the "Ja" is.

"John, it's time to go into the other room," I state, wanting him to react.

"John." I don't want to provoke him, but I'm not sure what his triggers or his tics are just yet. She left without giving me any information about his personality, his likes, or his needs. All of these things are essential to his care. Damn it.

"John, are you hungry?"

"Food."

A knock on the conference room door brings Rebecca, my boss and the head SPED councilor at the school. "Hey, Nora. The woman that just left dropped this off with the receptionist. She said she forgot to give this to you." She hands me a large envelope that feels like it has everything I'd need for John in it.

"Okay, thanks."

I want to open it right now, but he takes that moment to look up at us. "Who is this little guy?"

"His name is John. She wants him to join our program." I suppose we finally shook him out of his focus, and now he realizes that Julia's gone. Panic strikes him, and he flips out.

Rebecca enters the room fully and slams the door shut, locking it so he can't run out. "Oh, no."

"It's okay, John. I'm Nora." I point to myself. He runs to a corner and ducks down, banging his head against the wall. Damn it. I approach slowly so he doesn't hurt himself.

The floors are carpeted just in case kids get a little out of control. I'd rather his meltdown happen there than against the wall, so I gingerly ease him to the floor as he fights me. I'm sure I'll have scratches and cuts, but these moments come with the job sometimes.

"It's okay, John. I promise I'm not going to hurt you." My voice remains calm and low. "No one is going to hurt you."

"Maybe I should call the cops."

"No," I shout, regretting it instantly. John screams.

"Sorry, sorry." I look at Rebecca. "She's a friend and asked me to look after him. Now, can you take out those papers and hand them to me?"

She takes them out, getting a glimpse at them as she does and gasps. "Nora, you've just become a mother."

"What?" My mouth falls open. When she said take him in, I expected that it would be temporary.

"These documents are court papers naming you, Nora Harrison, the legal guardian of John Matthew Ingram, age five." I guffaw in pure shock, which for some odd reason makes John snuggle into me. Then I feel something rolling over my body. I tip my head and see John is using my torso like a racetrack for his car. His vehicle uses my boobs as hills before going down again.

"At least he's calmed down," Rebecca says.

"I guess so." When she asked me, she didn't plan on taking no for an answer.

"There's a list of his favorite meals in here, and he has no food or medical allergies. He isn't on any medications at present."

"That's very good to know. I don't want to try to take him out of the room yet. Can you have lunch brought in to us, so I can feed him and see if maybe a little more bonding can happen?"

"Absolutely."

AS PROMISED, A CAR SEAT IS DELIVERED TO THE office via a courier before the school day is over. Rebecca generously helps me install it while John allows me to buckle him in without a meltdown, which I call a major win. Although, the car ride to my house is a nightmare because he cries halfway there, trying to get out. Thankfully, he isn't able to get out of the special harness.

My nerves are shot by the time we pull into my driveway. I press my head to the steering wheel, wanting to cry, but I hold myself together. An overwhelming sense of defeat fighting to take over me is unmistakable, but I've been there before—I didn't let it then, and I wouldn't let it now.

Just as I'm about to lift my head, someone pounds on my car window, startling me. With a gasp, I jump back to see Julia.

"Hurry. You shouldn't be out here just taking your time with him in the open. It's dangerous," she gasps. She goes around to the back passenger door, and I unlock it. Quickly she frees John from his seat, and he clings to her. "Let's go inside."

"Okay, okay. Did they follow you here?" I asked, looking around frantically.

"So far they haven't, but I don't want them to get any ideas. Your school surveillance cameras were down today for maintenance, and that's why I used today to drop John off. I'm completely serious about his safety, Nora. I would give my life for him."

"I understand." I truly do, now more than ever. She is scared, and I can see it. As I reach for my front door, it's already unlocked. "Oh, no. Someone—"

"It was me. Go in." We enter my home, and I'm floored. It's as if I walked into someone else's home. The place isn't the same way I left it this morning, just like my life. Everything has been rearranged.

"Sorry, but I needed to make sure John has a secure place to live. It needed to be redecorated and safe. Your office is now here. Your desk has locks now so he can't get inside, and the keys are on the shelf." I am as equally impressed as I am pissed.

"How did you...?" I questioned.

"I had a little bit of help." There is so much more to her, and it scares me. "I know you have a million questions and fears, but it's for the best that you leave it all alone. Trust me when I say that the less you know, the better. John needs a good home and a loving mother to care for him. As much as I'd love to stay, the longer I'm here, the more likely he'll be in danger." She looks nervously around.

"But…"

"Don't worry. I've erased all ties to my transfer of him. It looks like I was never involved in the guardianship, and for good reason. These people are evil to want to kill a five-year-old harmless child." Her voice cracks with her honesty.

"Why are you doing this now, though?"

"I'm dying. I have advanced ALS. I'm not going to last long, and I can't take care of John, especially the way he needs to be. He needs someone to treasure and love him like a real family would."

I know that family means nothing, and they'd betray you just for a power alliance. After all, mine planned an arranged marriage with an Irish mob family. They wanted me to marry a man I didn't know who was thirteen years older than me, and Julia was the only one to save me from it.

I nod. "Yes, I understand. I accept, and I will protect him." With one last hug, she hands him over to me and leaves, never to step foot in my home again.

I finally turn my phone on and realize I have a voice message from Jeremy.

Hey, babe, I know things have been bad. I'm sorry. I want to talk about it, but I'm going out of town for the weekend to see my parents. Hehe. I hear a faint feminine giggle in the background. *Shush. So, we'll talk when I get back. I'll miss you.*

The bastard thinks I'm dumb. Shaking my head, I send him a text that it's over and that he can spend his time away with his giggling girlfriend. I'm not interested in a relationship. Once that's done, I toss my phone on the counter and carry on with my evening. Jeremy doesn't matter to me anymore because I have a child to care for and don't have any time for a cheating boyfriend.

Honestly, I don't have time for anyone, including myself.

"John, it's just you and me, buddy."

CHAPTER SIX

JACK

June 2013

"You need to stop obsessing over your brother. There are so many things to worry about, including the fucking governor." My blood pressure flies through the roof with those words, and I have him pinned to the wall with my hand on his collar, staring the old man down. I want to tear his head off. His common sense and fear had left him if he thought it was smart to let that stupid shit leave his mouth.

"Are you serious right now? Did you just tell me to forget about looking for your son—my little brother?" I snarl, teeth gnashing like a damn wild animal. The man has a serious lack of self-preservation.

Luckily for him, his men are there, and I won't pull the trigger with too many itchy trigger fingers around. Not to mention, I don't have the proof I need to say he was involved. If I get any inkling he was involved with my brother's kidnapping, he'll be dead. It's been two months, and we haven't heard a word or found his nanny yet.

"The kidnappers haven't contacted us, and the nanny hasn't surfaced in her usual spots."

"It's been two fucking months, and you're just going to give up?" I asked, disgusted by his willingness to quit. I released him with a shove.

He adjusts his suit, giving his men a look to stand down which is motherfucking wise because my men will end all of them before they try. "No, but I can't keep thinking about it or I'll go insane, and every damn enemy we have will strike. You can't be a damn leader if you let everything get to you. You look weak, Jack."

"Family is everything, Father, or have you forgotten?"

"I haven't. I just know when to act. I still have people searching for clues every day, but that doesn't mean I don't go about my day."

"He's five, and he needs us."

"Yes, and if he's still alive, they're taking care to keep him that way, so be cautious and keep yourself alive so that you can take care of him when you do find him." He has a point. If my enemies notice that I'm so damn distracted, they'll put a bullet in my head, but that doesn't mean I'm giving up my search. My biggest search is still his nanny. I have to find her before it's too late.

"Fine. I will. Now get the fuck out of here. I have things to do that don't require your presence." I escort my father out and as I do, my phone rings.

I close my front door and then I answer my brother Connor's call. "What's going on?"

"I got a lead on the nanny."

My heart pounds in my ears with that news. "What?"

"Yeah, we found her. She's holed up in an apartment on the West Side." So, she's in Chicago? That's a fucking miracle. She's either got to be stupid or up to something.

"Is John with her?"

"No. There's no sign of him anywhere, but we'll get the answers from her one way or another," he says, the darkness in his tone reminding me of myself, and I know that he'll string her up. Ordinarily we don't harm women, but for her, we'd make an exception.

"No, I want to get them."

Connor understands the chain of command, but it's more than that. I love John the most, and it's my fault he was taken. "Of course, Brother. I'll be waiting for you."

"Good. Bring her to the cell, and I'll deal with her."

"If that's what you want. We'll have her there shortly."

I'm out of the house in a matter of minutes, forgetting all of my plans for the day because the contact I was going to see had been about her anyway. I take the drive to the cell on the Northwest side of the city where we can privately interrogate people under the train tracks, and no one is any wiser. The sounds of my victims' cries are muffled from outside noises. It also helps that I jam all electronics in the area so no recording devices can capture my dirty work in the building as well.

Although, this torture I look forward to administering.

My driver pulls into the warehouse, and I see her tied to a chair with Connor standing to the side with his arms folded and waiting for me. "You got here just in time, Brother. I've been running out of patience for this bitch to talk. She stole our little brother."

"We don't know that. All we know is that she was taken with those thugs, but if she was involved, she'll pay." I storm up to the older woman with venom in my heart, ready for the torture to begin. She attempts to move backward in the chair, but it's futile since she's tied down. "What happened to my little brother? Where is John?"

"I don't know what you're talking about. I escaped those crazy men," she lies and she does it well. It's almost hard to tell.

"So you abandoned my brother."

"No. They separated us."

"Don't fucking lie to me," I roar. My hand is in her hair, slamming her head back. "He's been gone for two months. I want him safe and home where he belongs. You better pray that he's alive, or I'll make your torture last for the next five years."

"What do you want him for?" she asks, staring into my eyes with such intent, like she's reading me.

"He's my little brother and everything to me, so you better tell me where he is," I warn her through clenched teeth.

"You didn't seem to care this entire time. He's better off away from this terrible family," she spat out.

I wipe my face. "How dare you? He needs his family. Who gave you the right to rip him from the people who loved him?"

She scoffs. "You're not going to see him ever again."

I shake my head, and my heart sinks deep into my gut. "Tell me he's alive," I roar, tears filling my eyes because that can't be true.

Her face softens as if she understands the pain her words are truly causing me. "You do love him, don't you?" she asks.

"Of course I do." Her head turns, and her eyes scan the room as if she's gauging the men around the room, but it's almost empty.

"He's better off without your father," she whispers.

I bend down, moving in closer because I don't want anyone else to hear what I'm going to ask. "I know. Is he alive?"

She gives the faintest nod. Before I can ask her, a shot is fired, and she's hit in the head. "Fuck," I shout, jumping back. My men and brother spin around to see my father with his gun aimed at the nanny.

"What the fuck did you do that for?" I roar, ready to tear his fucking head off.

"She killed your brother."

"No, she didn't. He's alive."

"What? Where is he?"

"We don't know. You are a fucking stupid bastard," I say, rushing toward him. "She was about to say. How could you do that? What the hell is wrong with you?

"Sorry. She was involved in his abduction and the death of our men in the first place. I just couldn't stand to see her face," he roared.

"You're sorry? You killed our only lead to our brother and your son. How could you be so reckless?"

"You don't want him to be found," Connor accuses him, stepping up beside me. We watch as his shoulders drop. The pride is all gone from the old man and there's a shift.

"Of course I want him found. He's the last bit of your mother I have. I want him found more than you know." He stares at the dead body of John's former nanny with watery eyes. The devastation is written in his gaze, but I refuse to give him another moment. I don't give a shit if he is sorry or not.

"Clean this up," I say, waving my hand toward her dead body. As I leave, my head ponders one thing. John is alive. My mission will be to find everything on the nanny, where she was staying and all those she got to know.

It takes my driver a few minutes to get her address since the men who have her information are in the building and without a signal, but finally we get it and head that way. Apparently, there is already a team dispatched there. I hadn't ordered them to go ahead, but it seems everyone is willing to jump the damn gun tonight.

As my men reach her apartment, it explodes, sending debris everywhere.

"Son of a bitch." I stay in the back of my SUV and watch from across the street as plumes of smoke and embers fill the air. I tell my driver, "Just drive."

"Where to, Boss?"

"Home. I need to be there when the police arrive for questioning." I lost any chance to find clues in her apartment, and the assholes who went in without checking for explosives better hope they're dead because they've just cost me the last bit of hope I had to find my brother.

If any of those fuckers survive, I'll end their lives for their failure. How dare they not check for traps before entering? They're about to pay the price if they haven't died already. I storm into my home and up to my bedroom, rattling my door so hard that I nearly splinter the fucker in two.

My brother is lost forever, and for a brief moment, I feel sympathy for Joanne. She didn't want my brother anywhere near my father, and that I understood. He claimed the cut my brother got before he was abducted was an accident because John got a hold of a kitchen knife, but I wasn't sure that was true, and even if it was that meant they weren't watching him.

The kitchen is a long way off from his bedroom and play area. There was no way in hell he had a chance unless several people weren't minding him. He doesn't eat in the kitchen, so it didn't make sense to me.

I doubt my father was involved in my brother's kidnapping, but I'm positive he's not as upset as he pretends to be. More digging needs to be done into the men who kidnapped my brother. There have been no leads on the white vans. There are so many of them littered throughout the city that my men are searching every single one for any trace, dent, or scratch that matches the ones in the video. My bet is they've been torched, painted, or sent to another state by now.

Long motherfucking gone.

Stressed and frustrated, I strip out of my suit and head to the bathroom to get clean. After I shower off the nanny's blood and change my clothes, I find six missed calls from Connor.

I call his annoyed ass back as I walk downstairs. "What's going on?"

"I'm just making sure you weren't in that fucking building," he says, chuckling with relief.

"Of course fucking not. I wasn't stupid enough to enter without checking."

"Good. I didn't think you would have underestimated her or who she's working with, but the emergency crews have surrounded the place. So many of our vehicles are there. It's going to be a shit storm when the governor gets word of this. We need to cover it up."

"Damn it. Whoever lives needs to go away."

"Already way ahead of you, Brother. They'll all be buried by tomorrow."

"I'm not giving up on John. I know he's alive. She told me he was better off without our family."

"That doesn't mean he's alive."

"Trust me. She made it clear that he was still alive, and she was about to tell me. He ruined it. Don't let him talk you out of believing it."

"I won't, but I want you to stay strong and remember that it may not result in a positive end." Connor's definitely being more levelheaded about it because he's not the one who feels guilt. He loves John, but he also doesn't want children, or the burden that comes with caring for them.

"Trust me. I want to find him. Dead or alive. I won't have him alone without his family."

There's a long sigh, and then Connor adds, "Jack, Dad's worried that they might have sold him to a trafficker."

"I doubt his nanny would do a thing like that." She didn't have it in her. That's what upsets me about her death. Above all, she loved John and my father ended her life for trying to take my brother away from a monster. I wish she would have come to me in the first place, but damn it, I would have at least protected them both.

"No, she wouldn't have, but maybe the person she gave him to might have."

"They'll die for it." I can't believe it. I refuse to, but I might not have a choice. Now that she's gone it won't be long until the person finds out and then John will be in serious danger.

For all around, he'd better be alive, or hell will be unleashed. Vengeance will be had. Every day that he's gone will be paid in spades. The longer he's gone, the viler I'll become.

I crack my knuckles and then walk over to the mini bar in my living room. Pouring myself two fingers of whiskey, I toss it back and think about where to begin. Her work history is going to be my first search, but unfortunately, the cops are going to be all over the area given the explosion at her place.

I don't waste any time and head to work, pushing open the doors to my study. My contacts need to be swift and cunning while continuing to search. Sliding into the chair behind my desk, I dial my brother Ian. "What's going on, Jack?"

"We found the nanny, and your asshole father killed her before she fucking told us where John was."

"I hate that bastard. He's never been a father to me." Ian and my father have always had tension between them. Ian didn't act like Connor or myself, so my father took it out on him. He always clung to my mother and then when he was a teen he rebelled. He never wore a suit and let his hair grow longer than my father cared for. Ian didn't give a shit, though. "Do you think he's involved?"

"I don't know. I've looked for any evidence, but nothing points directly to him, although I have nothing that says he isn't involved either. Where are you?"

"I'm in Vegas, enjoying myself for the weekend."

"Well, have a good time. I'm going to head to bed before the police show up here in the morning. I have a feeling they'll be looking for me with questions about vehicles and dead bodies."

"Let me know if you need me for anything. Anything at all."

"I will." I end the call, staring at the screen on my computer. It's a picture of John and me. He's not facing the camera, but it's the best picture I have because I'm happy. I remember that day because it was the first time he hugged me for no reason. If only he'd learn to speak, it would be wonderful.

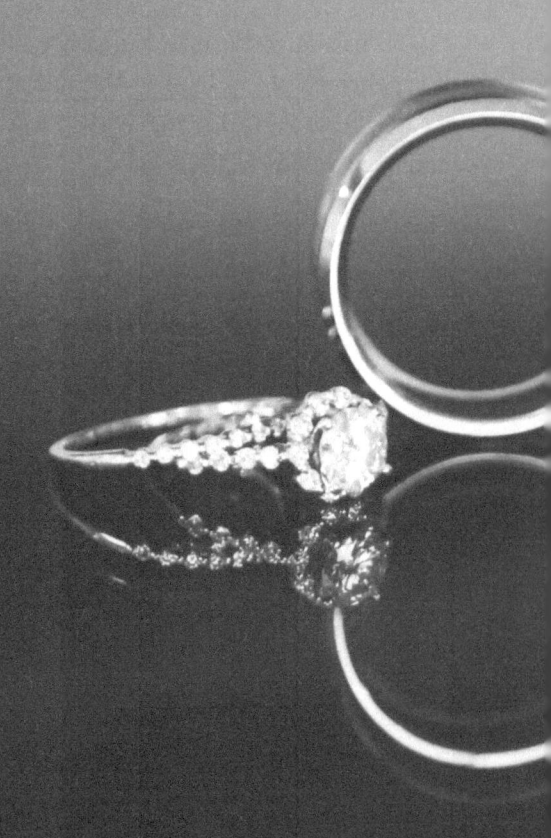

CHAPTER SEVEN

NORA

JUNE 2013

"With your new obligations, Miss Harrison, we know this is difficult. If you need help, please let us know." I stare at the principal with a bit of shame, wondering how obvious it is that I'm drowning. My outfits aren't as on point as they were, and my lack of sleep has started to show on my face. If I were better at putting on makeup, maybe I could hide it, but that would require time, something I'm surely lacking.

"Thank you. I appreciate it," I say, my eyes moving to the left of her where John plays on the floor with large building blocks. He's by himself because the school day has ended, but I needed a break and let him play for a while longer with no interruption. The principal leaves the area and Rebecca comes back, anxious about the brief meeting. Everyone is aware of the situation because it was the talk of the entire building, and of course I had to have a meeting with the administration about it.

"Any word from his mother?" she asks.

I look back at her and shake my head. "No, and it looks like I'm now his permanent guardian." It's been weeks since Julia left John in my care and disappeared. She uprooted my life and my home, leaving me in complete chaos.

"Yes. I didn't mean… it's just, I wondered if she would come back." Did my face give away my apprehension? Julia made it clear that she wasn't coming back, and it had to do with John's safety.

Thankfully, as teachers, we're good at masking our emotions because I frown and say, "I believe she was ill, and that's why." I couldn't tell her the full truth, of course. It wasn't like I could say that he's the son of a dead mobster and his family wanted him eighty-sixed.

"That's terrible. Well, you're going to do a wonderful job, even if you don't believe it, Nora." She rubs my arm, giving it a gentle squeeze before releasing it. "You're a great teacher and a sweet, loving person."

John looks up at me and drops his block. I read the tension building in him. "Thank you. I should go." She follows my gaze and does her best to smile at him, but he's already avoiding our eyes. Damn it. Can he sense my mood? He's a smart boy, and I'm already certain that other people's emotions affect him immediately.

"John, sweetie. We have two more minutes, and then it's time to go and have some dinner." My voice is soft and upbeat. Rebecca and I begin to clean up the last bit of toys in the room.

As we get to the last pile, I say, "One more minute," hoping John understands me. He's had several meltdowns over the past few days, but thankfully, we were able to coax him into a calm state. He's not particularly violent with other kids, but he's aggressive with his body, flailing and tugging on his hair. I want to hold him and tell him it will be okay, but I don't know if we're in danger.

The school year ends soon, and it will be just the two of us at home for the entire summer. I can't imagine what I'm going to do with him. Because we teach the special education programs, they only have one program for the summer, and it's a partial day that doesn't begin for weeks and it's only a three-week session. I don't want to disrupt his schedule once I get him into a summer routine, so I might not want to do it.

"Okay, John. It's time to go." He doesn't look at me, but he gets up when I put my hand out, which is a wonderful start. After a quick bathroom break, I gather his light jacket and our things, and we drive home. On the way there, I turn on music and pay attention to which songs seem to make him happy or upset him.

He definitely prefers rock or pop music at a medium volume. I make a mental note of it and plan to add a playlist to my phone. When he's settled in, I make him some mac and cheese and help him into his chair. He has a problem sitting still, so we sit together, and I wait to eat dinner because I've learned that my food will get cold. I'm not sure if it's a mom thing or an autistic mom thing. Either way, moms endure a lot, and it's going to be a rough ride.

After I put him to bed, I stare at the paperwork in front of me. Nowhere is there contact information for Julia or her legal name. Everything here is under my name and John's. It labels me as his legal guardian after the death of his parents.

I look up the Ingram family and find they died six months ago in Newark, New Jersey with no other family except some distant relatives in Europe. So, she must have worked for a family out of the country and fled back here when this all happened. I don't understand anything other than the boy has a scar on his face that is healing, and he's clung to me, making it difficult to do the smart thing and take him to the police.

Even if I do, everything here shows he is legally my child, but I have no experience other than my education and my minimal hours as a paraprofessional. My two-bedroom house has been quickly remodeled into a home for a child with extra needs.

The doorbell rings, sending little John scurrying behind me with his voice letting out a squeal. Damn it. I slam my eyes shut and hope the person at the door goes away because I'm not in the mood for solicitors. I didn't invite anyone, and no one ever just pops by. The doorbell rings again, dinging repeatedly.

"Nora, what's going on? Your car is in the driveway." Shit. It's my ex-boyfriend, Jeremy. Damn it. How am I supposed to deal with him right now?

"Um. Jeremy, what are you doing here?" I ask through the door. I've been avoiding him since our terrible date.

"I was driving by and saw your car." My brow arches and my chest pounds; my life has become a whirlwind of chaos. How did I end up with a child? A child with special needs that, although I'm capable of handling in short bursts, I'm not sure I'm qualified for it as a full-time job.

"Nora, are you going to let me in?" His tone is demanding.

"You need to go. We're not together anymore. I broke up with you, or did you forget last month?"

"I'm sorry. Give me a moment to talk." He continues to knock, which upsets John. Shit. I decide it's best to answer the door before he breaks it down. I can't risk the cops coming here with John and asking more questions.

I take John to his bedroom and sit him down, making sure he's secure before locking the gate on the door. "I'll be right back," I whisper to him before rushing toward the front door.

As I open it, Jeremy pushes his way in. "Whoa, Jeremy." I press my hand against his chest. "What are you doing?"

"You've been avoiding me." He moves around my hand and moves to the middle of my living room. I grab the handle of the front door.

"I think it's best you leave."

John starts crying from his bedroom. I slam my eyes shut, afraid of what's going to happen.

"You have a kid here?"

"Yes, I'm taking care of a friend's kid for a short time."

"So, you have time for someone else's kid, but no time for me." Wow, what a fucking child. I can't remember what I ever saw in him that made me agree to go out with the bastard.

"I'm sorry, but yes, that's the case."

"God, you're such a bitch. When you get rid of the little brat, give me a call." He storms out of the house with a shove against my shoulder. I lock the door quickly and then check on John, who thankfully is playing with his toys without a problem.

I breathe a sigh of relief as I hear his vehicle drive off. Goodness, I hope Jeremy remains a problem of the past. There is no way I can handle him in my life now. If he shows up again, I'll have to call the cops.

CHAPTER EIGHT

JACK

June 2014

I slide off my ruined button-down shirt and toss it into the fireplace. "Fuck," I grumble as I watched another two-hundred-dollar shirt burn. I've gone through more suits than I care to admit in the past year of searching for my little brother. Still, I'd go through a thousand more just to get him back.

Most of the time, I manage to change before I go on a hunt for my brother when I learn of a possible lead, but unfortunately, the traffic ring was on the move, so I had to move quickly. Rushing in, I took off the heads of the bastards who held two dozen boys and girls for sale.

As I looked at all the kids, none of them were my brother, but I still called the authorities and took off without a trace. This has been my tenth fucking raid on a child trafficking ring. It's sick as hell, and yet I'm grateful that John hasn't been found there.

Still, I need to find him. All the nanny's ties have come up empty. She changed her name shortly after the kidnapping and attack, but there was no trace of her movement until that time between. She must have planned everything out perfectly, or everything we needed was in that apartment and was blown to pieces, completely lost to the fire. This woman had someone helping her hide her identity and they were good at keeping it a mystery.

Changing into a clean suit, I go out to meet with my investors on a new commercial building. "Thank you for joining us, Mr. MacNamara," Franklin Simons says, shaking my hand.

"You're welcome. I'm always looking for good investments," I say as if I wasn't just dealing with the scum of the Earth.

"Let's take a look at the numbers. I have the report from the inspector, and there aren't any concerns since it's a brand-new construction."

"That's good news." We spend a good two hours talking about the project before heading out to lunch. As I leave the restaurant, I run into my father, who is dining with a random woman younger than me as if he has no cares in the world. It irks the fuck out of me. I've been running around doing everything I can to find my brother and he's trying to seduce a younger woman.

He pretends to not notice me with intent, of course, because he wants to sleep with her. She's only after his money, so it's not like he can't pull it off. I plan to interrupt for fun because I hate the bastard.

"Hello, Father. Who is this?" I give her a wicked smile. As if I have any desire in knowing this woman. As far as I'm concerned, she's nothing but trash to be tossed in the dumpster out back for dealing with a man like my father. I have very little respect for gold diggers, and less for ones who fuck with my father.

"You have a son?" she asks, looking up at me with sensual interest.

"Four, actually," I add, pulling up a chair from the table across from them. The patron looks like he wants to say something, but then quickly bites his tongue when he sees me. He clearly understands what's good for him.

"So, what are you doing with my father?" I questioned, staring at the two of them with contempt. It's a gorgeous day out and he's with a woman more than thirty years younger.

"Enjoying a nice lunch," she says, smiling at me over her glass. I'm growing angrier by the moment.

"Son, this is Detective Lopez. She's looking into your brother's case." My father doesn't get the satisfaction he's looking for because I mask my surprise.

"Well, it's a true pleasure to meet you, Ms. Lopez, although I can't say you're that good if you didn't know he had sons."

"I wasn't supposed to reveal my status just yet. Apparently, your father was to keep that quiet so that we could learn who was involved in your brother's abduction."

"I told you, my two oldest would have nothing to do with it," my father says. I'm about to kick the chair from out under him.

"None of your sons had anything to do with it," I bark out. "Ian's the one who was worried something was wrong at the estate. He wanted to turn around that morning because he felt the atmosphere had changed. He called me and asked me to check on the property because he was in Vegas on business. It's the reason he had to leave. If his flight wasn't early, he almost canceled it, but the meeting was important."

"When did he call you?" she asks. I can see her puzzling the situation in her head, but she better not consider Ian a suspect. He's the last person I'd ever imagine would hurt John.

"He called me as soon as he landed, but I was in a meeting so my assistant let me know when I had a free moment."

"What did he tell you?" We have nothing to hide and if she's truly there to help I'll give her all the information. I'm sure my asshole father spun it so that Ian looked guilty.

"That it seemed too quiet. There were less guards patrolling, and no one was around in the morning. It almost didn't feel like the property was alive. I told him that we were already out handling business, and maybe

John was still in bed so the guards were light for a reason."

"Then what?" I'm starting to get annoyed with the damn questions.

"He asked me to check on it."

"That's it?"

"Yes, why? You can't think my brother had anything to do with it," I exclaimed.

"No, I'm guessing the same thing. I saw the footage, and it shows the property looks uneventful. All three of you leave at different times, and nothing happens. No guards are seen throughout the cameras until the time of the explosion."

"What do you mean, no guards are seen?" Did I miss something? Was there more I hadn't noticed? Damn it. I need to re-evaluate the footage. I'd been looking so close to the kidnapping I'd lost interest in the hours before the abduction.

"Well, I mean there are a few passing by, but not more than two or three until the attack, and then everyone comes in to fight." That I understood. The men came from their stations after the explosion at the front gate.

"They fought and did their job, but unfortunately my brother and the nanny were still taken." The detective's phone rings and she excuses herself from the table, explaining that she has to take the call. We nod, and she leaves us.

My father leans forward and says, "The nanny had to be involved."

"I think she saved him from the kidnappers, but she never gave up anything before she died," I recall. I haven't forgotten the words that she uttered before my father came in and pulled the trigger.

Of course, he had no idea that she was about to tell me that my brother was alive and where I could find him. I knew she was about to confirm what she had only nodded, but he stole the answers from right in front of me that day. All he had was the hate in his heart for the woman and her betrayal. She read the hurt in my eyes, and for a brief moment, we were on the same page.

For an instant, I believed I would get the answers I'd been searching for, only for her to be silenced forever and my brother to remain lost. I couldn't imagine where he was or who had him. The damage that was being inflicted on him scared me. No, it terrified me. I wanted to kill her for letting this happen and yet, I had no recourse, no avenue, and my poor helpless brother was out there in the world with God knew who. If it wouldn't show our enemies a weakness in our house, I'd end the old bastard for his failures.

I glare at the man who made any answers impossible to get. "That's because you killed her before we got any information. If you'd given her another minute, I would have had an idea where to find him."

"I was fucking furious. She'd betrayed me, and I lost it. Who knows if he's alive. She would have just lied to us to try and spare her life only to find a way to escape on our way to find John." He had a fair point, and the only reason I hadn't pulled the trigger first was that I needed information that I would have dragged out of the older woman even if I had to torture her all day and night. I was good at torture. No, I was great at it and I would have made it my mission to get the answers I needed.

This discussion is pointless. I have shed my vitriol over the past year many times, and it has done no good. "What are you doing here anyway?" I ask.

"I heard rumors that the governor is making waves again." Another fuck who I hate as much as my own flesh and blood.

"Maybe stop having a pissing match every time you two encounter each other, and then he wouldn't be digging for shit." I don't need the added problems my father decided to bring when he bumped heads with the governor.

The man already has an inflated ego after getting elected illegally. This state is corrupt as fuck, so it's nothing new that he's one step away from being as guilty as us. It's not like he doesn't commit crimes, but he's smooth about keeping it secret. Unlike my father, who wants to just display his mess in the old politician's face like a giant *you can't touch me—fuck you.*

"I hate the bastard."

I nod, acknowledging the resentment, but not caring because I have more important matters that take precedence. "Understood. I'll investigate his activities and get back to you on it. Is there anything else? I have a meeting to attend that requires my full attention."

"Don't let this slip by. The governor is getting too ballsy and can be a major problem."

"Understood. Now, if you'll excuse me." I take leave of my father and do my best to ignore whatever he has to say.

I can't handle his nonsense or even look at his face and not want to break his jaw as I'm still thinking about what happened to my brother. It's his fault, and I want him to pay for my brother's disappearance. For nearly two months, I believed my little brother was dead, and then I learned he was alive. Then, my father killed the only fucking person who could tell me where my brother could be found.

All I want to do is beat his brains in. I pass by his detective as she looks at me with her mouth open. I wonder what she's up to. Something in me screams that she's not really investigating my brother's abduction. My guess is she's working to get at the fucking governor because that's all my father cares about. I'll find out one way or another.

My driver opens the door for me, and I slide into the back of my SUV. Just as he does, my phone rings. "Fuck. Another interruption. Sometimes these things are a nuisance." I take it out of my inner pocket, and it's Giles. I haven't heard from him in a long while. The last time was when I sent the entire crew a picture of my brother and asked them to be on the lookout for anyone trying to claim the small boy as their own.

"What's new, Giles?" He's probably interested in an investment deal.

"It's the strangest thing. I know I haven't seen your family in a long time, and maybe it's out of place, but I'm handling business in Philly right now." He pauses, and that irks me more than it should. After having dealt with my asshole father, I'm just a little on edge.

"And?"

"Well, I know your brother's missing." My heart is in my throat. "And you sent us the picture of him." He pauses again.

"Get to the point, Giles."

"There's a little boy with this woman, and he looks like John. I know little boys look alike at this age, but she called him John, and, well…"

"I need a picture."

"I snapped a quick shot, and I'm sending it now."

"What else?" Every nerve ending in my body activates, adrenaline pumping with excitement as the possibility of a sighting. It could be a mistaken identity, but there is a chance it's my little brother.

"Well, he caught my attention because he threw a fit in the middle of the street." My phone dings with the notification and I check the image from Giles. I'm staring at the blurry photo from the shot he captured of the boy who could totally be my brother. He looks to be about the right age even though the boy is a little taller and healthier. Still, over a year of searching for him and my attention isn't on his image. It's the woman holding him that draws my attention. She's gorgeous and has spectacular hips. Who the fuck is she? Why does she have my brother?

Pressing my phone to my chest, I slam my hand on the glass and command my driver, "Stop. Turn around and go to the house." We were supposed to head back to the office, but nothing else matters when it comes to John.

"Giles, don't confront them because I don't want them to run, but I want you to find out who is with them and where they're staying."

"Yes, Mr. MacNamara."

"And Giles?"

"Yes?"

"Not a word to anyone. Not even to my family."

"Understood."

"You will be rewarded well if this is my little brother." I get to the house and step out of the vehicle, turning to my driver and head of my personal security, Shamus. "Get ready. We leave in thirty for the airport."

He doesn't ask stupid questions. "Business or pleasure?"

"Both."

"Okay. I'll be back shortly." I nod and step into the house with my phone in hand, calling my brother, Connor.

"Connor, I need you to handle the dealing at Warehouse 42 by yourself."

"What happened to you?" Normally it doesn't take two of us to handle a large shipment of guns, but we had other matters to discuss afterward, so I agreed to go with him after I stopped at the office.

"Something's come up. I'm leaving town and won't be back for a bit," I say.

"Anything serious? Anything you need my help with?"

I'd love to tell him, but I'm afraid of getting his hopes up and I frankly don't trust anyone around that woman. After what my father did to the nanny, I can't let anyone near this little thief with my brother. "Not yet. I'll let you know soon. Hold down everything for me. You're my second. I can count on you for anything, right?"

"Always. We're brothers to the end."

"Good. I'll be back soon. I might be calling on you, but until then, I need you to keep tabs on Father and make sure he stays here. If he leaves the compound, let me know instantly."

"Of course. You don't trust him for shit. Does this have to do with John?" He knows me too damn well.

"May be a lead, but I have to be sure, and I don't need that trigger-happy bitch ruining anything."

"I'll keep that fucker here and maybe put a bullet in his head myself if he tries to leave."

"Good. By the way, he was meeting with a detective. A little young piece of ass. She tried to hide that she was cop for some stupid fucking reason, but he was quick to throw it in my face that he was getting help to look for John's kidnappers."

"Interesting. I'll check into it." I'm sure he will. I wonder what my father is really up to because I doubt it has anything to do with John.

"They were interested in Ian."

"I'll be definitely watching out, then. Let's just keep this to ourselves for now. We don't need Ian going apeshit crazy." Connor's not going to mention it to Ian because my younger brother is a hot head and might just slice that bitch's throat for good measure.

"Good." I end the call and finish packing a suitcase, and then I call my pilot. "Marty, I need the plane ready and running within the next two hours."

"How many passengers?"

"For the FAA, three. In reality, six. The return flight, we'll change it up. I can't say how long we'll take."

"Where's the destination?"

"Philly."

"Okay. I'll be fueled and ready in an hour." I want to be up in the air within the next two hours. Realistically, an hour isn't possible because of city traffic. It's going to take forever for me to get to the bloody airport.

Philly's a short flight away, but it already feels like an eternity. My hand goes to my phone and back to the picture. I zoom in, but it doesn't focus the image any better. He's at an angle and it's been so long since I've seen my little brother, but it's got to be him.

My heart thumps in my chest, pounding erratically. I have to know if it's truly him and who this woman is.

Since I learned that he was alive, I've traveled from town to town, checking shelters, foster homes, and freed little boys from predator dens because I was searching for my brother. Every sick fuck I found in those debauchery dens paid for their sins with the end of my gun or blade. I enjoyed those kills more than anything ever. Each kill was a reminder that someone could be hurting John the same way.

Shamus calls on one of the other guards, Frankie, to drive us to the airport. We ride out to the private tarmac, and I receive another image from Giles of her license plate. I drink a bottle of water. I want a fucking whiskey, but I need a clear head. I don't know what to do with this information because I don't run plates, and I can't call my sources without drawing attention to this woman. I need to be close to her first, or rather, close to John.

We land in Philadelphia around seven at night, and I want to pound on the woman's front door, but I don't have any of her information yet. Giles meets us at the hotel about an hour later.

"What the fuck took you so long?" I questioned. He knew when we'd be arriving at the airport, so he should have been ready to go. My usual cool, calm demeanor fades when it comes to this pursuit. Knowing that we finally have visual evidence of John, I can't hold back much longer. Every moment feels like an eternity.

"Sorry, I was watching her home to see if there was any additional movement, and then I got a business call that required my attention. I wasn't expecting you so soon," he apologizes.

"No, you're right. Did you get any more details, photos?"

He nods. "Yes, and I dug a little deeper and went into her mailbox while she was taking the kid into the house. Her name is Nora Harrison."

He hands me his phone, and there's a dozen more photos; there's no doubt that the boy in her arms is my little brother. He looks healthy and clings to this woman as if she's his lifeline, so I know he's being taken care of, but that's not the fucking point. She stole him from his family, robbing him of the love and life he deserves for no damn reason. If she wanted a baby so damn bad, I would have gladly put one in her fucking belly.

Whoa, where did that shit come from?

I shake my head and hand the phone over to him. "We need to get him tonight." My face focuses on the photos, wondering where I've seen her before. I don't even know if I have, but there's something familiar about her features. She's beautiful without a doubt, but there's more. I recognize her, although I can't say from where or when.

"I think it's best to wait. Sleep, and then you can strike first thing in the morning. Don't you want to learn more about her before you go in?" Giles asks.

"How am I supposed to do that without alerting her?" I asked.

"Do you think she's that sophisticated as to have her name flagged?"

"How about if someone watches the house, and we'll pull the records so if she tries to run, we'll be there," Shamus adds.

"Sounds good, but I really don't want to wait. I say a four a.m. attack is better."

"A blitz attack?" Giles remarks, drinking a beer from the hotel fridge.

"Yeah, but then she's more than likely going to call the police than answer the door," Shamus says. That's true. If she's wise she'd call the police before we made it through the door, but I'd nab her ass before they got there. Still, I don't want to frighten John.

"True. I don't fucking like any of this." He manages to hold me off to a reasonable hour, but I can't sleep as I wait for any report on this woman.

It finally comes in, and I learn a little more about this thief. She's a twenty-four-year-old teacher who isn't married and has no children. No fucking children, so she shouldn't be carrying an obvious child with her.

I didn't sleep for more than an hour, wearing out the rug in the hotel suite. When the time was right, I hollered at these lazy assholes to get up. Shamus was going with me while Giles stayed back in the driveway just in case she tried to run.

We pull up to the quaint little house and I find it strangely inviting. If I didn't know better, I would assume a good person lived here. However, I am aware of what this woman is. She's a thief who stole my little brother and tried to keep him as her own. I step out of the vehicle and quietly close the door to make my approach to the front door smooth and silent. Damn, the sun is just rising and the temperature feels like it's burning me up. I tug at my collar, feeling the damn heat. She needs a shady tree in front to block all the sun. That was a stupid thought and I'm not sure where that came from. Maybe it's the lack of sleep or the frustration of being so close and yet so far.

"Ready, boss?"

"Yes." I crack my knuckles and approach the door. "Now, it's time to get my brother and deal with this woman." My hand raises, and I pound on the door.

CHAPTER NINE

NORA

June 2014

"Nora, I'm totally sorry that today was a bust. I thought you two would do good with an outing. You needed it," Rebecca says. She's been so supportive for the past year, and I couldn't have done it without her. She's been the rock that I've needed to get through all the stressful times.

"I did, but it was more stress than it was worth." My head pounds as I fight back tears. It has been a rough day.

John's screams had nearly broken me, but I managed to hold it together long enough to get him out of the mall and into the car without looking like I abducted the child. Goodness, the irony of that wouldn't have been lost on me. Yes, I have the papers saying that he legally belongs to me, but how he'd been placed in my care never felt legal.

"I told you that I would have watched him for you." Rebecca is a saint, but I can't rely on her generosity, especially when there's an unknown danger lurking out there. I'd hate for her to fall victim to it because I wanted a reprieve. Rebecca becoming a target was unacceptable to me.

"No, I couldn't let you do that. John isn't good with anyone when I'm not around." Honestly, after what happened at the mall, I knew it was better to have kept him with me.

"You won't even believe how much worse it was. I ran into Jeremy while I was there," I exclaimed. That was just as rough as the fits John was throwing.

"Are you serious?" she gasps. We both know my relationship with Jeremy didn't end on good terms. He tried calling and working things out, but with John, I hadn't even given it a second thought. That ship sailed before I met the adorable little boy.

"Yes. He saw me as I was coming out with John. He walked with me to the car and actually helped with getting John in his seat. It's as if he cared for a brief moment." It was nice to have that little help, but I hoped he didn't take it as a sign that I wanted him in my life again.

"Oh, girl, please don't take that as a sign to let him back into your life. I know it's hard with John now, but you don't need a cheating piece of crap like Jeremy in it."

"Oh, heck, no. I have no interest in letting him in. Seriously, I'd slam the door in his face if he dared to bring any relationship up. He cheated on me, and we're done, so there's nothing left for us. I ended things. It just reminded me that I was alone. How long will that be?" I sighed. I hadn't wanted a relationship, per se, but I sure as hell didn't want to spend my life alone either.

"Well, if you ever let someone else help with John, you might be able to date," she huffs, sounding perturbed.

"Fine, girl. Maybe soon." She was right. I needed something, some sort of companionship because I felt like I was losing my mind. A year of almost pure isolation had gotten harder to handle. Before John, I had some friends and I went out to stores, the movies, even the bookstore. Now, all shopping is done online, and my friends have all but disappeared. Rebecca being the last to stick around.

"Good. Because I want you to be happy. You're one of the only friends I've got."

"Same here, girlie. I need you too."

"Well, call me anytime." We hang up, and I think about the outing.

I got an extremely uncomfortable feeling today when I took John to the mall. What possessed me to be brave enough to shop in public, I'll never know. It had been dumb. Maybe it was the need for human interaction, or just pure insanity. Whatever it was, I felt someone's eyes on me.

I think I've grown completely paranoid. Julia's fears have seeped into my soul, and now I'm searching for monsters at every entrance. It's not like they'd come looking for

John all the way in Philly. It's the reason she brought him here instead of taking him to Chicago where we were from in the first place.

Her godson had lost his parents in New Jersey, and his family wanted the boy dead as well. It was crazy, but she let them believe the boy was already dead, so there was no reason for them to look for him in my neck of the woods. Besides, I haven't heard from Julia since the day she left him with me after registering him with all the paperwork, leaving me as his legal guardian. How the hell she managed to pull that fast one surprised me, but she had secrets I didn't know about. A lot of them.

"Momma," John whines through the baby monitor I have next to my bed. It's cute and draining as I sigh and slide out of bed because it's well past midnight when I hear his cries. As much as I love teaching special needs children, I never expected that I'd suddenly become a full-time mom overnight at twenty-three.

It's harder than anything in the world. No one prepares you for the reality of it. My kiddos at school go home to someone else. Someone with patience, who can share the burden and the joy. I don't have a family or a husband. I no longer have friends or a boyfriend. His cheating ass is long gone and I'm glad for it because the last call I got from him, he said I should send John off to the state. The guy was a total prick, but that doesn't mean that I don't ache for someone to help or even someone to talk to.

"What's up, buddy?" Seeing his face makes me forget that I'm worn out.

He cries, reaching out for me. I hug him and realize that he needs reassurance. It's been ongoing, and I wonder if he's always been like this or if it has to do with Julia and the loss of his parents. I close my eyes and hold him tight. I would take him back to my bed, but I refuse to make it a habit. Routines must be followed. "Time for bed, John. Do you want a story?" I use the sign for a book, and he nods.

After two stories, he falls back to sleep, and I quietly sneak out of his room and onto the sofa where I pass out until there's a loud pounding on my front door that startles me awake and sends me to the floor.

"Hold on," I say in a shout and then remember that John's in the other room. "Fuck," I hiss, standing up and dumping the covers back on the sofa. I'm hoping whoever is knocking like they're the police didn't wake him. Shit, I hope Jeremy didn't think yesterday was a way to worm his way back into my life.

"Do you have a problem?" I ask as I whip the door open. My eyes land on a large chest in a suit and as I lift them upward, I'm met with a furious expression of a handsome man, and then he storms into my home. He has his hand on my throat, pushing me into the house. Before I can fight back, I'm pinned to the backside of the sofa with one hand on my throat and the other on the cushion, giving me nowhere to go.

"Where the hell is he?" he snarls. Beautiful, stormy eyes stare dangerously into mine with an intensity that I can't fight.

"Who?" I choke out, gripping his wrist and trying to pull it away, staring into the gorgeous blue eyes of a killer. The dark way he looks at me tells me all I need to know. He doesn't play and he means business, and yet a part of me isn't as scared as I should be until he utters the next syllable.

"John," he grits out, eyes narrowing. My heart sinks. They've caught me, and he's coming to hurt the poor, innocent little boy.

"I don't know what you're talking about," I lie, trying to protect him like I promised. There's nothing I wouldn't do for him and that means fighting to the death to protect him.

His voice gets deeper, lower. "Don't play dumb with me." I shake my head. "The little boy you had yesterday." Shit, I was being watched. I knew something felt off.

"I'm a teacher. I had a day trip with a student," I lie again. He releases his grip and then he moves around me, sees the toys on the floor, and looks up at me with a deadly smirk. I dash around the room and block the hallway. My small body isn't going to hold him back for long, but I'll do whatever I have to do to protect John. Why is it so damn important? The kid isn't going to say anything.

"Momma, ma...." John whines from his room, and I know he's on his way.

He roars, "You lying little bitch." He storms toward me until there's no space between us.

"I'm not..."

He grips my shoulders, ready to pull me away, but he doesn't use any force. "If you don't want me to kill you, get the fuck out of the way."

"I won't let you hurt him."

His eyes shift lower. "Hurt him? I'd never fucking hurt him." His pearly white teeth clench together so tightly that I swear they're going to crack. The words he spat back were as if I insulted his character. A man who shoved his way through my door, put his hands on me, and threatened my life—looked at me with disgust because I accused him of wanting to harm a little boy. It would be almost comical if I wasn't terrified that he would.

I sigh as I hear the pitter-patter of John's little feet because John's out of his room and has walked straight into danger.

He drops to his haunches with his face right at my crotch as he stares at John. "John, buddy, do you remember me? It's Jack." There's no anger or violence in his tone like there was for me a moment ago. He sounds so happy and so calm. His voice cracked at the end.

"Jack," he answers. I heard him say it when we'd watch television, especially when there's a man in a suit, but I didn't think anything of it or put two and two together. "Jack, Jack." I see this big brute that just threatened me with deadly bodily harm begin to sob.

"Yes, buddy. It's me. Jack." He opens his arms, but John doesn't go to him. He clings to my leg. The brute stands and looks at me with tears in his eyes. "What the fuck did you do to my brother? Why do you have him?" He fists my hair violently, so hard that I let out a cry, and it causes John to cry.

"You're scaring him," I yell at the big asshole. I don't care how good looking he is with his angular jaw, cleft chin, and the touch of gray at the closely shaved sides of his head. The damage he's doing to John is pissing me off. *Whoa, where did that come from? Why is this man turning me on when I should be petrified? He's what I've been hiding from for the past year.*

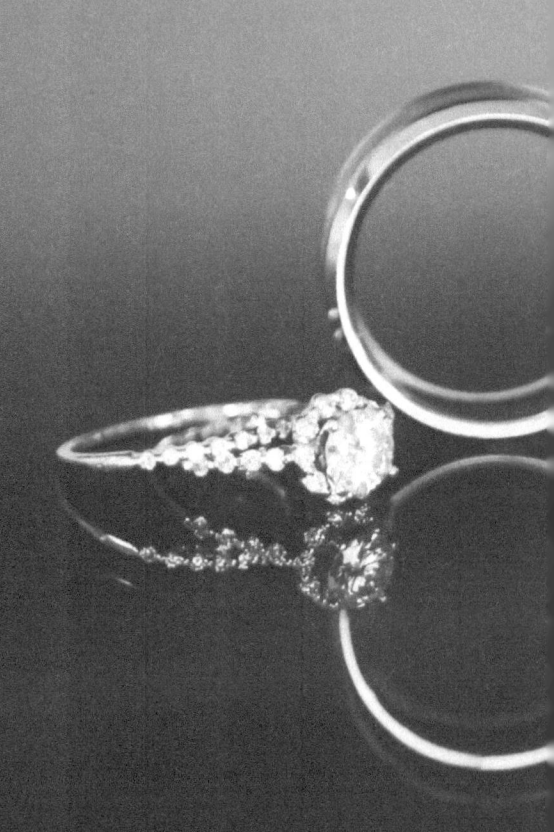

CHAPTER TEN

JACK

I STEP CLOSER, GIVING HER NO SPACE, PARTIALLY to stop her from getting away and to get a little more of her scent. The little dark-brown-haired beauty with hints of red in her hair stares at me with a bit of fear and hunger in those tired but beautiful greenish-brown eyes. Why does she look so damn familiar?

Breathing her in, I stare into her gorgeous hazel eyes and challenge her, wanting her, needing Nora to show me who she really is. "Scaring him? You stole him, terrified him for so long, and I'm the one he should be afraid of?"

"I've done nothing but look out for him while you've been hunting him down like a dog, wanting him dead." I'd be proud of her bravery if it wasn't for her insult to my love for my little brother. It's so damn disgusting that all the desire I felt a minute ago has passed.

I twist my head to the side, face tightening, hands at my sides flexing into white-knuckled fists. "Want him dead? Are you fucking nuts? I get that you're fucking sleep deprived from the dark circles under your eyes, but I would never do anything to hurt my brother."

She's practically spitting fire for that intentional dig, but I need a little reprieve from the instant attraction I'm feeling. This woman kidnapped my brother, and I should string her up for what she's done, not want to drive my cock deep inside her hole and stay there until we both can't move.

"I'm just supposed to believe you after you burst through my door, violently threatening me," she challenges me. Damn, does she challenge me. I want to take her young ass over my knee and spank her. Who the hell does she think she is, talking to me like that?

"Little felon, you don't know what you're talking about."

"I'm not afraid of you." She's lying, but Nora's not going down without a fight. What kind of woman would give her life for a stranger's kid?

"You need to be afraid." God, even sleep deprived, she's stunning. The dark circles under her eyes don't take away the beauty, but that doesn't change my plans. I want my brother home where he belongs.

"You stole my brother. For one year, two months, and three days."

"I didn't—" My hand wraps around her delicate little throat, unwilling to believe her lies. I really could get used to that feeling. Her pulse under my fingers, vibrating violently, is intense and erotic. What would it feel like if she was riding my cock at the same time? *Damn it, Jack. Shake it off.*

"Don't fucking lie to me, ever, little felon." I breathe her in and groan. A mixture of distrust and desire bleed through me. What am I going to do with her?

The answer pops out of my mouth before I can think of a better one. "John responds to you, and you clearly respond so well to me. For your crimes, you will be John's mother and my wife, my little felon." She gasps and I smirk, stepping back.

"You have to be out of your mind. I'm not responding to you at all." Another fucking lie out of that gorgeous, pouty mouth.

"I already warned you about lying," I say, staring into Nora's striking hazel eyes that scream longing. I'm not sure what she's longing for, but I'm willing to satisfy her.

"Momma," John cries at her side, clinging to her desperately.

"Come on, let us relax." I turn to my men while still holding on to my future wife. "Stand down and wait over there. I have a lot to discuss with Ms. Harrison. Make yourselves useful and get her some water."

"I..." It's adorable that she thinks that I'll be persuaded to listen to her. Leading her over to the sofa, John follows her before going to his toy bins. As her ass hits the cushions, fatigue falls over her. I almost feel bad that I came barging in—almost.

As I reach up to brush her cheek, she flinches. I should be offended, but then again, I've threatened her more than once. "You need to relax. It's clear that my arrival disrupted your sleep." I caress her soft skin briefly before she moves her face away.

"Relax? Are you freaking serious? You barge into my home, threatening me and John."

"I've never threatened my little brother," I inform her. I'd give my life for him. "You took him from me."

"I didn't do any such thing." She huffs, looking adorable and so familiar. I wonder if Joanne chose her because Nora has a much closer connection. Trying to picture Joanne's appearance, I look for any similarities, but I'm not seeing it. John returns to Nora with a toy in hand and climbs onto her lap without any permission, invading her personal space. He straddles her body, clinging to her.

"How the fuck did you end up with him in your care, and why is he calling you Momma?" I growl, feeling the insult to my mother since the title belonged to her, even though I'm thrilled that he's speaking at all.

"Look, I didn't kidnap him. I was asked to look after him even when others told me to send him off to the state." My brow kicks up and my hackles raise. Who the fuck else is involved? They'll lose their lives for that shit.

"Who told you to send him to the state?" he growls. "Your boyfriend?" That fucker needs a bullet in his head and in his dick for good measure.

"Well, ex, now." That's very good.

"He thought my brother should have gone to the state?" I want to snap the fucker in half. Anyone who thinks less of my brother doesn't deserve to live. He's a wonderfully special little boy who has struggles, but he's good. The only good one of us MacNamaras, and I hate how anyone could treat him badly.

"Yeah. I was twenty-three and just started using my teaching degree with no parenting experience, and raising a five-year-old autistic child is quite difficult."

"Autistic? John's autistic?" I questioned.

"You didn't know that? How could you not know that if you're his brother?" She jumps off the sofa, holds him tightly to her chest to shield him from me.

I press my palms up, trying to calm the scared mare. "It's not what you think."

"Oh yeah? She was frightened when she brought him to me, begging me to look after him, telling me he was in danger from his own family."

"I would give my life for my little brother. I've been looking for his kidnappers since the day it happened." She slowly takes a seat as John gets heavy in her arms. She sets him down and he runs to his toy bin again for another toy. "If I hadn't found her, I would have never known John was alive."

"Where is she?" she questions.

Fuck. I can't lie to Nora, or she won't trust me. "Dead."

"You killed her." She's off the couch instantly and my hand is on her wrist, dragging her down.

I answer as calmly as possible. "No. My father did."

Nora breathes deeply, attempting to regain her composure. God, she's beautiful. "When?"

"Last year." John climbs back onto her lap which she easily assists without even looking as if she's done it a hundred times.

Her judgmental gaze narrows at me, and I sense she's about to be fired up. "And you took this long to find him?" Who the hell does she think she is? And why am I so damn aroused?

Normally I'd tell her to mind her damn business, but seeing as she'll be my wife and I want her to comply, I may as well answer her with a basic response. I replied, "She never had a chance to answer before he killed her."

She purses her lips, studying me with questions. My little brother tugs on her chin, vying for her attention. Naturally she gives it to him, cradling his body tighter without breaking eye contact with me as if it's just automatic. He rests his head on her shoulder, playing with her hair and rocking. He used to do that with me before he fell asleep. Fuck, my heart feels that to the core. I want that again.

"He's still tired," I say, knowing his little quirks.

"Yes. He normally sleeps a little later, but you startled him awake."

"My apologies. I was quite anxious to see him and afraid you got wind of my arrival and were on the run."

"I've never heard of you. In fact, I don't know your name, other than Jack. As it is, all I know is that John's name was listed under John Matthew Ingram."

"Our family name is MacNamara." Nora's eyes widen as if she'd heard it before, but then she flinches again.

"John, please let go." I realize he's tugging on her hair. I reach over and help free his grip and say, "How about you lay him back down so we can talk for a bit? There's a lot to discuss, and I'd rather do it while he sleeps."

"I believe that would be a good idea. Hopefully he'll agree." She gives me a halfhearted smile. I remembered that a lot of the stuff we were allowed to do with John depended on his mood. An involuntary chuckle comes from me as I relive those days. To think that was considered a better time.

As we stand up, I look around the room and wonder if John's old nanny gave her money, or if she just gave John all she had. Her house is small, not more than two bedrooms, a bathroom, and a medium-sized kitchen with a small living area. It's modest but clean, even with all of John's toys lying about.

I look at my men and point to the toys. "Clean up the toys." They tip their chins and then get to work, putting the toys in the bins near the television. We walk to his room, which is set up nicely for a teacher's salary. She sets him down and I cover him, giving him a kiss on his forehead. "I've missed you so much. I'll never let anything happen to you again, buddy."

When I stand, I find her eyes on me and try to ignore the sensual desire that runs through me. My family has always been a priority for me, and I would never deny my feelings for them. Everyone knows what they mean to me, and anyone that harms them learns that I'm serious.

"I watch you with him and I see your sincerity, but it still doesn't explain why you didn't know he was autistic. Your suits are expensive. The clothes he came with cost more than I make in a year."

I nod. To her it screams of neglect, but it couldn't be further from the truth. "My mother's birth was difficult. We were told that his birth was complicated, and he suffered brain damage during the process." Nora gasps. The sound causes John to move slightly in his bed, and we both look at him. Giving each other a knowing look, I take her by the forearm and lead her out of the bedroom.

We go into the hallway, and I continue. "My mother died less than a week later. My father never grew attached to my brother because of it, but my other brothers and I did. However, when it came to getting more treatment for him, that was my father's choice, and his doctors all agreed with my father that it was the brain damage he received at birth."

"Couldn't you have fought for custody?"

"Sweetheart, do I look like I go through legal channels? The only way things happen in my world are through force. Now, things have changed," I say, growling out that last bit. My father isn't getting an opportunity to choose. John is mine now.

"So is your father…"

"No, he's very much alive, but I'm curious what John's nanny told you."

"Nothing, really." Nora shakes her head.

I wrap my hand around her throat, knowing it turns both of us on. Fuck, my dick is hard as I watch the way her eyes brighten up and her pulse races. "What did I tell you about lying to me?"

"Look, it was over a year ago, so it isn't all that damn clear. All I know is that I've been afraid to take him out except for school because she said that his family would be willing to kill him and that his parents were killed….and he was her godson."

CHAPTER ELEVEN

NORA

HE FREES ME WITH A SMIRK. "AND YOU JUST fucking believed that shit? How fucking gullible are you?"

I chuckle hard and shake my head, wanting to kick him in the shins. "What's your proof he's your brother? Just because he knows your name doesn't mean anything."

"You know that's a lie. He's not like a regular six-year-old boy, so don't bullshit me. John doesn't even speak, or at least he didn't." He has a point, but I just want to be a bitch right back.

"Hold on a second, you jerk." I walk into my bedroom, and thankfully he doesn't go past the doorframe. Something about him following me in would be a little too intimate. I was able to put a small desk in here to do some work where John couldn't touch. Opening a locked drawer, I pull out a folder.

I walk over to him and push the file folder against his chest. "These are filed with the court, so trying to shred them won't do anything. I wasn't being naïve. She provided me with these."

He takes a few steps back into the hallway and I close the door, locking it. "You lock the door?"

"Yes. I try to keep John from getting into things." Why am I afraid of his opinion? Not like he's going to be angry, but like he's going to judge me negatively.

"Smart," he answers with a nod. It makes me smile, but I quickly mask it and hide my face by tucking my chin and crossing my arms. It doesn't matter because Jack busies himself by leaning against the wall with the papers in his hand, reading them with a scowl on his face.

It takes a few minutes, but he reads the documents and with each page his face grows darker and darker. "These may be legal in a sense, but they're all fake papers."

"What do you mean?" I question. I didn't have any rights to John this entire time.

"First off, his name isn't John Ingram. His name is John MacNamara. The Ingram family," he says with a scoff of disgust. "Hell, that's about the only thing on here that's accurate, except that my mother is dead."

"Okay. So, she pretty much lied about everything." MacNamara... Could he really be Jack MacNamara of the MacNamara family of Chicago? She lied about everything, then; they weren't from New Jersey. I knew he felt familiar. We never met, but I knew of him and his name. I knew of his father—the reason I ran away.

"I don't know who orchestrated the kidnapping of my brother or why. To this day, everything is a mess. I would have gotten answers if my father hadn't killed her in a fit of rage."

I press my hand on his forearm, trying to calm him down. "If it was all a lie, why did she kidnap him in the first place?" I questioned.

"It could have been a ransom gone wrong," he mutters, thinking out loud.

"Since she escaped with him, the kidnappers failed, and it never worked."

"Yes, or maybe she was the kidnapper, and her cohorts lost their guts and bailed."

"Either way, I only met your brother when she brought him to the school I work at," I informed him.

"How did you know her?" he asks.

"We used to be neighbors when I was a kid."

His brows raise. "That's peculiar."

"I thought so too." His phone rings, and then he excuses himself. I take the time to check on John, who fidgets in his sleep. I should prepare his breakfast because it won't be much longer and then he'll be up. So, I head into the living room area and see that it's neatly cleaned up, causing me to gasp.

"I thought you could use a hand." He's removed his jacket, and now he rolls up his sleeves. My eyes move directly to his strong, corded biceps. Embarrassed, I quickly lift my gaze back to his.

"Does John still eat pancakes for breakfast?"

"Yes." My heart and head can't make sense of what's happening, but I just go with it because frankly I don't have a choice. My home has been invaded by four large men, and one of them makes me want to strip completely naked the second he looks at me. When he puts his hands on me, I'm practically melting in his arms, which is crazy because each time has been in anger. I've spent my life hating men like him, revolted by their actions, and yet the moment he looks into my eyes, I ache for more.

He sticks out his hand, waiting for me to take it. I do, and he leads me into the kitchen. "Well, I'll get them started. Would you like some coffee and a real breakfast for yourself?" I want to say no, but my stomach answers for me, gurgling like the bad pipes in this hundred-year-old home.

I let go of his warm and strangely safe touch and then pull out the pre-mixed batter from the fridge. "You already have some ready?"

"There are a few things that I can count on. If there are things I can do to make my life easier, I do it."

"I'm not judging; I'm just curious. That's pretty damn smart." He watches me as I move around.

Jack whips out his phone and calls someone. "Giles, pick up a hearty breakfast for six, please. Yes, the address you gave me yesterday." He ends the call, giving me a smile.

Pressing my hands on the kitchen sink, I ask my handsome intruder, "So how did you find me?"

"By chance, actually. An associate of mine happened to be strolling about when he saw you with John and recognized him and his behavior. He wondered if it was him and sent me a photo."

"Wow. The first time I took him out in public, and we were spotted."

"Quite serendipitous," he says. He takes the spatula from me and then pulls out a kitchen chair. "Now, please sit down. You look as if you have no legs to stand on anymore."

"I can make him breakfast."

"And so can I. Trust me when I say that it's truly my pleasure, Nora. I've waited so long to do something so mundane as this for him." I stare at him in wonder. He's different than I ever imagined. I was seventeen, almost eighteen, when I found out that we would have been married. Now I'm twenty-four.

"Why are you staring at me like that?" he asked.

"Are you bi-polar or something?"

He lets out a deep, hearty chuckle as he sets the pancake on a plate. "Please explain."

"You are dark, broody, and dangerous, and then you're this." I wave at the pancake-flipping, smiling man.

"What's this?" He gives me a crooked smile and a well-arched brow. He gets my meaning, but I know he wants me to say it.

"Like what a typical, hot family man should be."

"You think I'm hot?" He knows damn well he's gorgeous.

"Ugh." I roll my eyes. He's at my side, lifting me to my feet and pinning me to the fridge in a blink of an eye.

"Beautiful little liar, I am not bi-polar. I'm a dangerous man, especially when it comes to those I love, and I'd do anything for my family." He runs the back of his hand down my cheek, sliding it over my jaw to my collarbone and down my arm. I shiver and meet his gaze. Our noses brush against each other, and then I hear footsteps behind us. "I definitely get to you, Nora. Don't lie to me anymore. It won't change anything, except to make me angry." His lips graze my cheek and then he pulls away.

CHAPTER TWELVE

JACK

"Boss, here's the food." Shamus enters, holding the bags. He's much larger than many of my other men, so when he enters the small house, he looks like a giant.

"Where's Giles?" I asked, since it was his task. I don't appreciate people handing off assignments without my permission.

"He had an errand to run this morning. He said he'll be back in a couple of hours, but he'll be available via text." Yes, I'd been so consumed by my business I'd forgotten that he'd been working here when I'd gotten the alert. Now, it's time to contact Connor and Ian. They need to know I've found our brother.

"Please eat. I'll get John." She sits down, and I hand her the trays of breakfast.

"I like this spot. This restaurant is right up the street and it's my favorite."

"Good. Enjoy. Give me one minute."

When I slip into his bedroom, he's still asleep. I gently sit on the edge of the bed and stare down at my little brother. God, I want to hold him in my arms and never let him go, but I know not to push my luck. My phone rings in my pocket, and John stirs. Shit. I had called Connor, but he was with Dad so I couldn't speak with him. I told him to call me when he was free.

"Hey, did you lose the tail?"

"Yes. I left his house. The detective stopped by, wondering if you had any clues. She knows you've been hunting down trafficking rings, so they think you're on another one. Is that the case?" I chuckled. Let that dumb cunt believe it if she wanted. I didn't trust her one bit, but my brother needed to know the truth.

"No, but I wanted to let you know that I found him," I say in a hushed whisper as if someone near him might hear.

"What? Please God, tell me he's alive." His voice is shaky.

"Yes. He's alive and healthy." I'm so grateful to Nora for that. I want to pull her in my arms and kiss her right at this moment just for that fact. Not to mention that I'm so eager to devour her sexy ass.

"Tell me you killed every piece of shit involved," he snarls.

I sigh and then lightly chuckle because I've been out for vengeance since they took him, but that's the farthest thing from my mind when it comes to Nora. There's no way I'd do anything to hurt her. Well, except when I spank that ass and tear up that pussy. "So far there's no piece of shit to be found. Only a woman who was handed a child to care for."

"What? And you believe it?" Connor roars. I understood his anger, but I needed to set things right before I showed up with Nora.

"If you see the way she cares for him and how good he's doing, you'd believe it."

He pauses before he says, "He's doing good?"

"He called me Jack."

"What?" I might not be able to see my brother's face, but I can hear the excitement in the single syllable.

"Yes."

And then he surprises me when I hear my brother's sobs on the phone. "I can't fucking believe it."

"Me either. She's truly a treasure."

"Bring him home. God, it's a fucking miracle. I won't tell Dad, but he will have to find out sooner or later." As much as I hate to admit it, he's right. Even if my father had nothing to do with my brother's disappearance, he wasn't a good father, so he won't get custody of John, but he's still his son and he deserves to know he's alive.

"I want John safely tucked into my home before I allow it," I insist because I didn't trust that overreacting bastard.

"Let me know what you need me to do, and it's done."

John stirs as I speak. "Hey, buddy. You're awake. Do you want pancakes?"

John's eyes widened and he flaps his hands. "Cay, cay."

"Did he just say that?" Connor asks.

"Yes, he did, Connor."

"Can you say Connor?" I ask John, putting the phone closer to him without trying to scare him.

"Er. Er," John says.

"Fuck, I'll take it," Connor sobs. "I'll take it. Damn what did she do to him?"

My chest fills with pride for my future wife. "She's actually a special needs teacher."

"What?"

"I know, and she's fucking beautiful," I state profoundly. Nora is the most beautiful woman in the world.

"Whoa, Jack. What's going on there? Are you telling me something?" There's suspicious humor in his voice, so I decided to lay it out for what it is. No need to hold back because I'm not changing my mind when it comes to Nora.

"I'm telling you I'd like to fuck her, and she'd be great to keep around to care for Jack. It's about time I took a wife, so she's perfect."

"At least it's better than the arranged marriage Father tried to set you up with all those years ago with the Fieri family."

"I'm glad I didn't accept that damn arranged marriage with the Fieri family all those years ago." I wouldn't have the woman I really want, and John wouldn't have the mother he truly needs.

"Um...is something wrong in here?" I turned around to see Nora standing in the doorway with her arms crossed. God, she's perfection. Her long hair is in a braid and hangs over her shoulder, looking so damn hot. I want to hold onto that fucker while I ride her from behind.

I clear my throat to answer, "Oh, he just woke up. I didn't want to rush him."

She moves past me and directly to him. "No problem. You want bites, John? Let's eat so we can change your clothes for the day and play." She makes some hand gestures. He claps and slides out of bed. She takes his hand to lead him into the kitchen, while I feel like a complete asshole.

I still have my brother on the phone, so I explain how she just coaxed him with the hand gestures. "She just used some sort of sign language with John, and he did it with her."

"I can't believe it. This is a fucking miracle. When are you flying back?"

"Tomorrow morning. I'm not wasting any more time; John belongs in his family home, and I have a wedding to plan while I find out who really put together this kidnapping. I know it wasn't just the nanny, and I have a hunch the pretty little teacher doesn't know who is involved."

"Give me her name, and I'll run her info."

"Don't worry, I already have people on it. Just get John's room ready at my home and prepare a room for my fiancée. As much as I want her in my bed, I won't push it just yet."

"Acting like a gentleman…that sounds…well, just like you."

"I'll talk to you later, Con. There's still a lot of shit to get together before we can leave."

"Okay. Bring him back safe, Bro." I end the call and tuck away my phone. Now to go check on them. When I step into the living room, I'm shocked by how destroyed it is. How the fuck did that happen?

"Sorry, Boss. He kind of threw a fit and tossed the bin over."

"You messed up his chaos," Nora says with a soft laugh of surrender. She's already resigned herself to his behavior and mess.

"So, he didn't want pancakes, I guess."

"He did. He took a bite and then took off for a moment. We're working on sitting at the table and eating, but he runs off and gets distracted. It's one step at a time. One thing to learn is to pick your battles." I nod, because she's right. There was so much yelling or just plain ignoring John when he wouldn't do what my father wanted.

"So how do you get through the day?"

"It's not easy, but we have a schedule, and he knows it, so it has become a little easier. The weekends become a little messier, but that's okay. At least I get a little break. He's without a routine, and I don't have to be on twenty-four hours."

"You needed help."

"It's not like I had much of a choice. The first time I took him out in public, besides to school, and your people spotted me. Wow, that came out totally wrong. I wasn't intentionally hiding him. Well, I was, but not because I was being cruel."

"I understand. If there's anything I can say about how he's been treated, he's been well taken care of."

"Thank you." She smiles lightly, a blush spreading over the apple of her cheeks. I wish we were alone; then I'd take her into my arms and test how far that blush spreads.

"Shamus, we need to be ready to depart by tomorrow morning."

"You're leaving?"

"We're all leaving, Nora. Did you think we'd stay here? Our home is back in Chicago where we belong." Ugh, this city is nothing compared to my hometown. I roll my eyes with disgust at the idea.

"Chicago? I don't want to go back there," she says, shivering at the notion, and I wonder how many ghosts haunt her.

"Sweetheart, is there a reason you're afraid to head back to the city?"

"I haven't been back since I was eighteen and I bought this house. Besides, I have two more days of school."

"Well, I'm sorry. We're leaving tomorrow, and it's not up for discussion. The school year is officially over for you and John, so you better call your bosses and tell them you're taking an unexpected trip to see your family in Chicago because that's where we're going."

She slams her tiny fists into my chest. "You're an asshole. You can't just uproot my life."

I grip them in one of mine. "If you want to stay, that's fine, but I'm not leaving without my brother."

Her pretty hazel eyes widened in dismay and hurt. "You can't take him away from me. He'll freak out."

"He will, or you will?" I ask with a wide grin.

"He will…"

I cup her chin a little forcefully and give it a good tug. "Don't lie to me, little felon. I know that he'll be upset, but so will you and like I said, I'm not leaving without you. So, come tomorrow, you're leaving with us and we're getting married." With a stomp of her foot, she storms into the kitchen. I hear the sink running and then the dishes, so I follow. "What are you doing?"

"As much as you've pissed me off, I can't leave this place a mess. Dishes in the sink will only create a chance for pests to invade." She's scrubbing them furiously and I find it comical. I want to slide up behind her and ease that tension she has radiating through her body.

"You're taking it better than I expected," I remarked with a teasing smile.

"Look—Julia feared for her life, and it's freaking clear she had a good reason for it, so it's only wise that I follow along like a good little girl." I can't imagine harming her, but I'm not going to lose the leverage I have.

Julia? Is there another woman involved? My mind goes straight to the detective. "Why did you call her Julia?"

"Because that's her name. Julia Sanchez."

"No, my brother's nanny was named Joanne Rodriguez." I open my phone and show her a picture of the woman who had been taking care of John since he was born.

"That's Julia." She points to the woman I've known as Joanne. How the fuck has she gone all that time as John's caregiver without us finding out her true identity?

"And how long were you neighbors?" I asked, wanting to know if it was a short time. She could have been lying to Nora and her real name is Joanne.

"From the time I was ten until she helped me run away just before I turned eighteen."

"Why don't you get started packing some of your things, and I'll have the guys get you some luggage for John's belongings. I was in such a hurry I'd completely forgotten to get those things." I lift my shoulders and say to my men, "Gentlemen, let's leave Ms. Harrison alone and go to the hotel and store. I'll be back this evening."

"Boss, are you sure we should leave her alone?" Shamus asked.

"She's been alone with John all this time. I'm not worried about her with him because she's not running anywhere, right?"

"Of course not. I'd never keep your brother from you again." I pull her into my arms and cup her chin, causing a soft gasp to leave her perfect cupid's bow lips. "That's a very good thing, beautiful." I drop my lips onto hers, tasting them briefly before pulling back to find her eyes closed and looking dangerously tempting. "Go on and get packed. Don't worry about John's things. We'll pack them. I don't want anyone touching your panties."

She slowly sucks in her bottom lip and then massages them over each other. "Yes, Jack."

"Good girl." I'm so damn hard that I could take her in the middle of the room standing straight up, but it's not the time or the place. And just in case I need a reminder, John comes rushing up to me, headbutting my crotch. "Fuck," I grunt, swallowing the pain.

Nora giggles and snorts while trying to get John off me, but he clings to my leg. "Sorry. He's feeling a bit clingy, I guess."

"No, he used to do that a long time ago, but he was shorter so it wasn't a big deal."

"I'll be back, and be a good boy for Mommy because Jack plans to put a baby in there soon." I toss her a wink over his head. It's not something I should be thinking about since I don't know shit about her; however, I can't help myself.

The way her messy ponytail sits on her head makes me want to fist it in my hands as I slide up behind her and drive my thick cock deep into her tight cunt. It's fucked where my thoughts are going, especially with my little brother clinging to me, but my little felon has me twisted.

"I've got to go. We're burning daylight." We exit the house, and I tell Shamus, "Take the second vehicle and go buy five suitcases. Anything else we'll pack later. We don't need to take the whole damn house. She can put it on the market, or we'll treat it as a mini-vacation spot. Although, I can't imagine choosing to stay here over a lavish hotel downtown. Afterward, I expect you to promptly return and keep an eye on her."

I'm going back to the hotel to dig into the rest of her profile and John's former nanny. As soon as I'm in my room, I call my contact who wanted to speak to me earlier, but I was busy. "This is MacNamara."

"I have some interesting details about Ms. Harrison, or should I call her Nora Fieri. She's the daughter of Enrico Fieri." Fuck. My mind spins and I stumble back, falling onto the chair. "MacNamara, you still there?"

"Yeah. What else you got?"

"She got the money for the house via an inheritance from her grandparents after running away and changing her name. There doesn't seem to be any contact between her and her family."

I don't doubt it. If they knew where she was, they'd marry her off to another family. An involuntary growl rips from my chest. The thought of someone else getting to touch her infuriates me so intensely that I slam my hand down on the window ledge.

"You okay, Boss?"

"Yes," I snarl. That's why she fucking ran away and changed her name. They were forcing her to get married to me. My Nora ran off rather than being married to me. That knowledge stings, but I try to remind myself that she was a little girl back then and had to be afraid of getting married to a stranger and maybe had dreams of something more.

Damn it, that's why she looked so familiar. I never met the younger Nora, but she has the same eyes as her brother, who I've done business with more than once. "Is there anything else on her?"

"No. Do you need something else, Boss?"

"Yes. I need you to look into a Julia Sanchez. She would have lived next door to the Fieris in Chicago. Remember—everything is discreet, and get back to me as soon as possible."

"Sure." After the call ends, I send over his payment. Then, I gather my things and check out of the damn hotel. What am I going to do with my little Fieri?

Then, it hits me: what if that bastard was involved in taking my brother and sending him to his sister? I call the bastard. "Fieri," he answers.

"This is Jack MacNamara."

"To what do I owe the pleasure of your call?"

"So, I just realized that your sister isn't married yet. Where is she?"

"Why the fuck do you care where my sister is? She's not involved in our lives anymore." His temper shoots through the roof fast.

"I'm just curious. After all, I had her offered to me as a wife years ago, and maybe it's time I start looking for one. I'm not getting any fucking younger."

"That's good and all, but my sister's off fucking limits. She doesn't want to marry into our world. Besides, that was our fathers making that stupid deal. Neither of you wanted it, and she deserves to be happy." What the fuck? I'm fucking insulted.

"Who says she couldn't be happy with me?"

"You can't make her happy because the last time I checked on her, she had a boyfriend."

I growl inwardly. "Well, you haven't checked recently."

"What the fuck does that mean?"

"It means that I happen to have met your lovely sister, and she and I hit it off very nicely, although I didn't know she changed her name. She failed to mention that little detail when she was keeping my brother from me."

"What? No. She wouldn't. Don't you dare hurt her."

"I wouldn't dare harm her, but if I find out that you had anything to do with his kidnapping, I'll forget that we ever had an alliance or that you're her brother." I end the call and leave the hotel room with my things. Getting to her house and into her bed is a priority because after John's asleep, I'll be sliding between her legs and marking my territory. Everyone will know that Nora Fieri belongs to Jack MacNamara.

Still, there's one more thing I need to grab to complete the package deal.

CHAPTER THIRTEEN

NORA

THEY'VE BEEN GONE FOR AN HOUR AND I'M ON pins and needles, wondering what's next. My home suddenly feels like it's closing in on me. John has been easy to get ready, but I had no idea where to start. The past six plus years of my life have been in this house. How am I supposed to just decide what I need and want to take with me?

I think to myself that this is just temporary because I'm paying for the time John was taken. Will it be the length of time John was gone? I'm guessing so.

While they're gone, I remember that I need to make an important call. I have to clean out everything at the school. Rebecca has keys and can let me in, so I give her a call and ask her to meet me at the school. There are things I need, plus I can't just walk out without some explanation. She's going to flip, but I have to give her some sort of truth. Rebecca deserves it.

I have John dressed for the day, so I slide him into his car seat without any trouble, taking a couple of toys for the car ride.

"Hey, what's going on? This can't wait until Monday?"

"No. It's kind of important."

"Girl, you're freaking me out. Is this about what happened at the mall? I know you had a rough time, but you seem like yourself." I hug her as I send John to his little play area.

"No. It's not like that at all, and I wish I could explain more, except to say that the woman who left John in my care lied about who he is and how he ended up in her care. He wasn't her ward, and his parents aren't both dead. He was kidnapped, and his brother has been on the hunt for him ever since. It was a lucky twist of fate that I was at the mall and I was spotted. They came for him, and they want him back."

"You do have legal custody, right?"

"The documents are forged. Everything in there was faked, and, well, he's not going to press charges, but he's demanding that I accompany him to help look after John as repayment for the fourteen months that his brother was taken."

"Oh my God."

"I know. It's crazy."

"No." She points behind me, and standing in the doorframe, leaning against it and looking sexy as hell, is Jack MacNamara.

"Hello, little felon. Didn't I tell you to stay at the house?"

"Yes, but I needed to clear out my things and let my boss know I was leaving."

"That could have been done in writing, and your things could have been sent." He shakes his head. When I look back at Rebecca, she's practically panting in heat.

"Whatever. I didn't want to leave her in the lurch as it is."

"We have so many things to do in a short time, Nora."

"Not if you took a day or two."

"I've waited long enough. I'd say, fourteen months now," he adds, giving me a knowing look. My eyes widen because he's not even the least bit afraid to mention our situation.

"I'm confused," Rebecca says, playing innocent.

"Oh. Ms. Harrison forgot to mention that my brother was stolen from me," he answers with an air of annoyance.

"Oh, my goodness. I wasn't aware of his abduction—only the legal adoption."

"Yeah. Like I told you, Jack and I've straightened it out." I huff, glaring at him.

"Even though she doesn't like me."

"I can't see what there's not to like," Rebecca purrs. I'm about to kick her in the shins.

"Sorry, I'm taken." He sneers and takes my hand.

John finally notices his big brother and shouts his name. "Jack, Jack." He grabs his hand and pulls him over to his play area.

Jack tilts his head with a devilish grin that reaches his blue eyes and says, "Well, since I'm preoccupied, pack your things. You have twenty minutes, my pretty little fiancée."

Rebecca mouths, "Wow, he's so hot," as Jack drops to the floor in his impeccably tailored suit.

"Come on. Help me so I can get out of here." It takes a little longer, but Jack doesn't complain again. When I do come to get them, Jack's reading him a story that John's totally not paying attention to and riding a toy car over the pages. However, the second Jack stops the story, John grunts and puts his hand back on the page to read. So, I guess he's sort of paying some attention.

"Look, John. It's time to go," he says, closing the book.

"No, no," he shouts. Rebecca and I give each other a knowing look after having years of experience in this.

"Five more minutes," I call out. Jack looks at me, and I nod. He smiles, opens the book again, and continues with his story.

"So, he's making you leave with him for John? Ha. Looks like he wants much more than that. You're a lucky girl.

He's so damn yummy, and I totally have some daddy issues to resolve."

"Get your own daddy. He's spoken for," I hiss.

A moment later, I feel Jack slide his hands around my waist. "Do you have what you need?"

"Yes," I gasp, pulling away from him. "We should get him ready to go. He doesn't have shoes on." I walk over and look for the missing shoes while Jack springs John onto his lap. "It's time to go."

"Go, go."

"Wow, I've heard him use a handful of words today. It's a miracle."

"It takes a lot to get them out. He only started using them this past month, so if you'd gotten here any sooner, you wouldn't have seen much of a change."

"He doesn't make any eye contact when you call his name."

"It may come in time."

"Let me help you carry these things," Rebecca offers. John is in Jack's arms while I gather my paperwork. As we step outside, he loads the truck, and I see that my car is gone. "Where's my vehicle?"

"I'm driving you back. Your car has been taken to the house." I give Rebecca a hug goodbye while Jack straps John in. He does it easily, and then I remember that he's probably done it many times before. He gives John a teddy bear and then he helps me into my seat before buckling me in.

"Sit your pretty butt down. Next time I tell you to stay put, you do it."

I roll my eyes, pretending not to be aroused by him. The man makes my core temp rise effortlessly, even when he's being an insufferable prick. I wave to Rebecca as we drive away. I'm going to miss my friend and job, and find tears welling up in my eyes.

"Relax, Nora. We can come back, or you can invite her to Chicago. I'm sure she'd enjoy it. There are plenty of daddies I can introduce her to," he says, giving me a wink.

"You heard?"

"She wasn't quiet, but I did miss your response."

"It was nothing."

"You're a bad liar. You shut her up, so it must have been something of value."

"You are so…" I roll my eyes and ignore him, looking out the window, refusing to give him what he wants. He's already gotten enough wins today.

"That's fine." We hit up a drive-thru and pick up dinner before going back to the house. When I get there, the men are in the house with five new suitcases. "Oh my. Those are large."

"I wanted to make sure you could fit enough of his things and yours. We can get more another time, but for now, I need you to eat and then we can pack a bit." We both take turns feeding John while eating our burgers and fries. John will only eat the fries and a chicken strip. He doesn't eat much, but I make sure he gets his chewable vitamins as well. He's growing just right despite his food choices.

It takes two hours to pack up my clothes and my important documents. Then, I go into John's room to find Jack has packed most of John's clothes.

"Do you want to take all his toys?"

"All of them?"

"Well, does he play with them?"

"No. There's an entire bin I was going to donate. That's why he tossed them out and doesn't like them mixed up." Jack huffs out a deep sigh. "Don't worry. I'll sort them and then we'll pack all his favorites."

He stops me with his hands cupping my face and stares down at me. "No, you're not doing any of that. We'll take them all. We have the luggage for a reason. You look tired, beautiful. You should get some sleep."

"Thanks for telling me I look like shit."

He chuckles, and the sound shocks my system, vibrating through my womanly parts. Why the hell is he so damn sexy? "I didn't say that, sugar. What I said is you need to get some rest. We will be leaving in the morning and he's ready to go to sleep, so I think it's best if we all lie down." His hand rests on my hip, giving it a squeeze, and I swear I can feel it in every part of my body. I look up in his eyes, and I wonder where he plans to sleep tonight. "Do you think you'll be safe in that room tonight?" he asks me. "Do you sleep in there with him?"

"He's fine. I close the door and leave the light on just in case he gets frightened."

"Okay. Well, then, let's get you ready for bed."

"I can get myself ready for bed. I'm a big girl. Are you guys going to be okay?"

"I think we can handle ourselves."

He walks me toward the bedroom and leans down, pressing his lips to my cheek. "Get some sleep."

"So damn bossy," I remark with more sass than I mean to give off.

"I am. Now get to bed." He taps my ass, and my body bursts with unfulfilled need.

"Careful there, mister."

"Good night, beautiful."

"Good night." He smirks at me and then I head into my room alone, closing the door behind me, doing my best not to invite him in. I don't know what's come over me; maybe it's the fact that he's insanely gorgeous and enticingly hot, but I want him to take me into his arms and make love to me all night long.

It's crazy because I know exactly the kind of man he is, and tomorrow he'll take control of my life completely, dragging me back to my father and to his—a place I swore I'd never go back to. Shaking off the stupid, lustful thoughts and the fears about tomorrow, I focus on tonight and how much I want to get some sleep.

Stripping out of my clothes, I head into my bathroom and turn on my shower because for the first time in a while, I can take a peaceful shower knowing that John has someone to watch over him. With a sigh, I let the water sluice over my body and let my muscles relax by closing my eyes and enjoying the peace. I don't know how long I'm in there, but suddenly my shower is interrupted by the cries coming from the other room. I knew it wouldn't last, quickly throwing a towel around my body and another on my hair.

I rush out of the bathroom and down the hall to John's room.

"What the fuck? I got him. Get the fuck back in your room and put some clothes on before I have to kill someone." I realize that both he and his men are there trying to calm John down who had woken up.

I quickly rushed back to change into my pajamas and came back out to check on John. Jack's eyes are on me just as he closes the bedroom door again. "He's fine. He's asleep now. You, on the other hand, need a spanking, young lady."

"You wouldn't dare."

"The hell I wouldn't." He stalks toward me, and I move backwards, my back hitting the wall until there's nothing separating us except for clothes. He clicks his tongue against his teeth. "What am I going to do with you? Running out of the room practically naked, soaking wet with a towel barely covering your fucking pussy, tits bouncing with every step. Looking absolutely fuckable."

I look down like a fool and notice that his cock has made a stiff impression on his slacks, begging to get out of his zipper. The damn thing must be like a bat in there. "Not my problem."

"You're going to help me with my problem when I strip you out of these poor excuses for pajamas and fuck the shit out of you until you're screaming my name and we wake John up again." I swallow hard. Feeling bold, I reach out and brush my hand along his chest, grateful that he lost his suit jacket so that he's only wearing his dress shirt.

"I'm a virgin."

"Excuse me?"

"Jeremy was my first boyfriend since I moved here. Well, technically, my first boyfriend ever, and I wasn't quite ready."

"Fuck, you're such a surprise," he answers with a chuckle. "It's time for bed."

He waits for me to get under the covers before he turns off the lights and walks out of the room.

CHAPTER FOURTEEN

JACK

I DECIDE TO SLEEP ON THE SOFA BECAUSE I WANT to keep a watchful eye on both of them, but I send my men to a hotel. They can check out of their rooms in the morning. The damn sofa looks comfortable for someone who is five feet tall, not someone who's six two and two hundred pounds. Still, every sound sends me out of my sleep and with my blades ready to defend them.

Unable to sleep, I go to check on them at six in the morning. John is still in a deep slumber, so I'm off to the sexy little felon in the next room. My runaway almost-bride is lying on her back, her pajama top rising to show her flat belly, and my dick hardens painfully.

She moans and sighs, "Jack." Slowly her hand glides over her right breast. Damn, my future wife is getting off in her sleep to thoughts of me. It would be much better if I took her straight there myself.

I take off my shirt and slide onto the bed. My fingers gently lift her top a little higher until her nipple is in my view. "Tell me you want me to suck on your perfect tits," I whisper.

"Yes," she moans in her slumber. My mouth lazily captures her nipple, sucking softly, and then she wakes up, trying to push me off her, but I just release her nipple and smile. "Oh my God. What are you doing?"

"What you asked for. Now relax and let me finish what you started." I tip my head back and nip on her breast. "Fuck, you're so responsive. I can't wait until I'm buried between your thighs."

"Jack, what if…" she asks, losing her train of thought as my hand slips under her pajama shorts. I cup her ass and give it a rough squeeze.

"Don't worry. I just checked on him. It's only six. Let me please you," I commanded. She needs to learn to submit to me for her own good. She nods. "Good girl. Time to get what you deserve and so desperately need." My hand moves around to her soaking wet pussy. She's covered in a light dusting of hair. I wonder if it matches her hair color, but I'll see in just a minute because even if she comes on my fingers, I'm not going to be done yet. I want her to soak my face before John wakes up.

She fidgets nervously. "Relax, or I will have to spank you."

"You're all talk, Mr. MacNamara."

"No, baby. I'm just trying to keep quiet for John's sake. Our mansion at home is much larger. He won't hear you scream as you get the spanking you deserve." I lick the underside of her breast, and her head falls back. "You are going to cream all over my fingers after I turn your ass red. Then I'm going to fuck you until you remember that I'm in charge."

"We'll see about that."

"Keep challenging me," I growl, and I bite down on her nipple. "I'm about to forget you're a virgin and tear through that hole." She clenches around my finger, enticed by getting railed, but I can't do it and then have to stop because John wakes up. "If I wasn't afraid of being interrupted, I would."

"You're a tease."

"You haven't seen anything yet. Wait until you defy me." I pump my finger into her perfect, wet hole, watching her body learn what she likes.

"Jack," she whispers.

"Tell me—are you going to be a good girl and come on my fingers like you should have years ago?"

"I…can't."

"Yes, you can." I take her lips with mine, kissing her tenderly as I add a second finger, and my beautiful fiancée comes undone, soaking my fingers with her first of many orgasms for me. Bringing them to my mouth, I lick my digits and suck the glistening fuckers clean.

Her head is flat on the pillow as she tries to get herself under control, but I'm nowhere near done. I want another.

It was too fast, and I only got a taste of her, a tiny sample. I need a feast.

"That was sweet, but where do you think you're going?"

"I should check on John."

"He's fine. It's only you and me in the house, and the house is locked up. He's still asleep, so stop trying to hide from me. Don't be embarrassed, because I'm so fucking turned on by your blush. The way you come is so sexy, but I want to see you do it again. I want to feel it, taste it as you do." With my hand on her chest, I nudge her back onto the pillow.

"You're wicked, Mr. MacNamara." Grabbing the cotton material, I pull her bottoms off her ass and down her slender legs. Fuck, her curls are a shade lighter than the hair on her head, and I'm somehow even more turned on. I part her thighs.

She attempts to close them, but I slam them wide open. "Keep them open for me unless I tell you otherwise." She gasps, but that sexy blush deepens. "That's right. You like being told what to do by me, and that's fine when it's only me." I press my thumb to the bottom of her slit and then swipe my tongue along it.

"Oh shit, wow." I eat her like I'm starving because I am. Fuck, I'm pissed that I've missed out on her cunt all these years. She should have been mine, tied to me, lying in my bed every night, getting her pussy tongued down. That jackass she was dating was so lucky he didn't fuck her because I'd kill him.

I dip my finger into her hole, stretching her out because I need to get her prepared for me. There's no way she will be today, though, because I'm too damn big for her virgin little cunt.

"Jack, Jack," she cries out, fisting my hair, running her hands up and down my neck and over my shoulders.

She clamps her hand over her mouth as she screams my name so loud that we both worry she's woken John up, but thankfully he doesn't stir more than a little movement in his bed. I pull back and swipe at my light beard. As much as I'd like to spend all morning giving her orgasms, I need to check on John.

"I'm going to wash up and check on John."

"I'll do it," I tell her. I head into the bathroom and wash my hands and face. When I get out, I slip on my shirt, but she's already out of the bedroom. I open the door, and John's in her arms. She's only wearing my button-down dress shirt, and she looks sexy as fuck in it.

"Time for breakfast, and then we're going to head to the airport."

"Okay." She seems less reserved than yesterday, but she's not ready to leave any more than she was before.

WE BOARD THE PLANE AND THANKFULLY, JOHN decides it's a good time for a nap. We are able to tuck him into a seat and settle him down easily after putting on a movie.

The flight attendant brings us each a drink, and my men sit on the other end of the plane while I speak with Nora, who's in a pair of shorts that did little to help my aching need to be inside her. *Damn summertime.*

The airplane is a cool sixty-nine degrees, but outside today it is eighty. When we land, I expect the humidity to smack us in the face, so the damn ridiculously short shorts were fair, but they're wreaking havoc on my blood pressure. Her long hair has been wrapped up in a tight ponytail, showcasing her sleek, slender neck that I want to suck on.

Reaching over, I cup her hand that's on her bouncing knee, lacing our fingers together. "I'm sorry that I'm taking you away from your life here."

She pulls her hand away, using it to grab her drink, taking a long gulp before setting it down shakily on the table between us. "Afraid of flying?"

"Um, no."

She's completely unsettled, and I refuse to keep this between us so I stare at her, waiting for her to let me in. It's only been two days, but there's some sort of instant connection between us that I can't deny. "Jack, can I be honest with you?"

I take her hand and hold it firmly so she doesn't pull it away. "Always. You know damn well I want your honesty."

Nora bites down on her bottom lip, bracing herself and working up the nerve for whatever little confession she's going to give me. I know the truth, so I just need her to spill the beans and unburden herself. "It's not that I love my life in Philly so much as I fear going back to Chicago."

"Does it have to do with the fact that you were supposed to marry me years ago, Miss Fieri?" I question with a bit of amusement in my tone because I'm unbothered by it.

She gasps, squeezing my hand, her color paling. It takes her a good moment to regain her composure and ask, "You know? How long?"

"I learned when I went to the hotel again. It looks like you were meant to be my wife one way or another."

"It seems you're getting your way," she huffs.

I chuckle. "No offense, beautiful, but I didn't want to marry you then either. I didn't even know about the supposed arranged marriage offer until the day before you ran away."

"Oh." Fuck, I've offended her. I reach out and cup her soft, feminine chin.

"Don't hide from me, Nora. If I had met you then, trust me when I say I would have made sure you didn't get away and you were carrying more than my last name by the end of the week."

"You're a smooth-talking man, Jack."

"No one would believe you if they heard that."

"Well, I'm glad that you saved it for me, then." I bring her hand to my lips and kiss it.

"We have a lot of planning to do for the wedding, but I don't want to wait a long time for it."

"How long?"

"No more than a month."

"Okay."

"I suppose you gave me a long enough time as it is," she teases.

"That I did."

When we arrive at the airport, my brothers are waiting for us. Their eyes widen when they see me carrying John. "Holy fuck, it's true." Ian's eyes fill with tears.

"Little man is back," Connor chuckles. He reaches out and rubs his hand. It's what he's always done. A little touch that John allowed. John lifts his head off me and toward them before dropping it to Nora, reaching for her with a whine.

"It's okay. I'll take him."

"He's too damn heavy for you. He can walk, or I'll carry him."

"So, you're Nora," Connor says, eyeing my future wife like a fucking vulture.

"Keep that tongue in your motherfucking mouth before I rip it out."

"Calm down, Brother. I only wanted to say thank you for taking care of John."

"Come on. We shouldn't be out in the open," Shamus says, looking around.

"He's right," Ian adds, putting his hand on Nora's back, leading her to the vehicle while watching out for trouble. As my head enforcer, it's his job to take motherfuckers out and protect the family.

"And, Nora, John looks very healthy," Connor said, "so whatever your part in this, I'm glad you took care of him."

"I told you she wasn't involved in the abduction," I snarl, buckling John into the car seat inside the SUV. Ian takes the driver's seat while Connor moves to the front passenger seat.

"Yes, but she's related to the Fieris."

"How did you know that?" she asks. I sit her on my lap and close the door.

"Because we've met before, haven't we?"

"Yes, we did," she answers. "I thought he was the one I was marrying."

Connor and I bust out laughing. "I was in the middle of killing someone."

"Oh, yeah, not a great first impression. Either way, I was out of there and told my dad I wasn't interested, but he wasn't having it."

"Father would have settled on any of us marrying her, but Fieri wanted you because it meant the king of the MacNamaras, the heir to the empire."

"Well, it doesn't mean shit because he is a drowned rat as far as I'm concerned." I take her hand and say, "He sent my bride running. Tell me, now, beautiful. Did he put his hands on you?"

"It was a long time ago." God, having her on my lap makes me fucking hard as hell.

"That's all I needed to know."

"You never have to be afraid again. You know that, right?" Connor says. "You're marrying this crazy fucker, and he's not going to let any shit like that stand. He's been hunting down every lead for John for the past year. Hell, he would have found him sooner if my stupid-ass father didn't lose his temper."

None of us miss Nora's visceral reaction at the mere mention of my father.

"What was that about, Nora?" Connor asks.

"Nothing."

"Don't lie to me," I growl.

"I didn't lie to you."

"Fucking semantics. We all saw your fucking reaction," I grunt, gripping her chin and making her look at me.

"Okay. I met him once, and he made my skin crawl."

"Wow, she must really know him," Ian chuckles.

"Don't worry. I won't let him harm you, and you don't have to deal with him if you don't want to. You're in charge of our household, and I'm the head of the family now—not my father."

"Oh, I thought he was."

"Not anymore. He hasn't been for several years now."

"Good. We don't have to see him today, do we?"

"No, we're going straight home." We pull into the estate and directly to my mansion and into the garage. I refuse to give my father even a glimpse at John. So far, he's unaware that we've found him.

"When are you going to tell him about John?"

"It won't be long until he comes to see me and learns of my wedding, so I may as well address the issue tomorrow. Giving us a day to settle in is the best way to go about it."

"That works, Brother. You know we're here for you all in every way." They help us out of the SUV and into the main foyer of the house.

"Welcome to your new home, Nora."

"John, you are home, buddy," I tell my little brother.

"Mr. MacNamara, you're back." Agnes, my housekeeper, comes into the hall with a big smile. Her mouth falls open at the sight of John and then at Nora.

"Oh, my goodness, I can't believe it."

"Yes, I found him, but it's a secret for now. Tomorrow we'll go see my father."

She nods. "Do you need anything? Mr. Connor prepared everything you requested, but I had no idea why."

"Let's show John to his room," Connor says. Ian and Connor grab their suitcases while I take him and one suitcase. Nora walks beside me.

Connor opens the room just down the hall from mine. It's further away from the stairs, so he won't be able to run down them without passing my room. "Do you want to see your room, buddy?" I ask him.

Ian opens the door, and it's set up sparsely and yet safely. "I read up on autism yesterday and thought you might want to decorate it with what you feel is safe."

"Thanks, Bro. I appreciate it very much."

"We brought a lot of his toys, which will help him acclimate. Thank you," Nora says. We open up the suitcases and as we get to a third, it's Nora's and I quickly zip it shut because her panties are in it. A growl slips past my lips.

"Jack, why don't you help Nora with her things? We can spend some time with our little brother. We haven't seen him in over a year either."

"Are you sure?" I ask them, because he can be too much at times and they had trouble before.

They smile and nod. "Of course. We missed him too."

"Okay. We won't be long."

"Take your time," Connor says, wagging his brows. Nora blushes, so I take her hand and her suitcase with me and lead her to our bedroom down the hall.

As soon as I have her in the room and the door closes, I pin her to it, my mouth slamming on hers. "Jack," she moans as I pull back.

"Woman, I've been waiting all day for that."

"Me too." My hands slide under her top. "Please," she begs.

"What do you need, babe?"

"I need you to touch me." I lift her top over her head and toss it on the floor, then scoop her off her feet, carrying her to the middle of the bed. I shrug off my suit jacket and toss it on the chair.

"Fuck, I'm going to touch you everywhere." Her tits bounce as her ass hits the mattress, and I'm salivating like a teen seeing his first fucking set. My dick is so damn hard that I might nut way too soon, but I can't do that to my woman. I bend down and slip off my shoes and socks, followed by hers until we're both barefoot and there's one less damn thing in our way.

My hands slip into Nora's hair, and I dip in for another taste of her lips, sliding my tongue along hers and tasting a bit of mint and chocolate. I groan, aching to just consume her, body and soul. My fingers move up and down until I cup her breasts through the fabric and swipe my tongue over the uncovered soft, plump tops.

She needs to be completely naked before I go insane. I reach around and unsnap her bra, freeing her luscious tits from their confines. Her breasts have to be the most spectacular things I've ever seen. I want to devour them. I'm never going to get any work done because every time I close my eyes, these beauties will be there. There won't be a moment where I won't be fantasizing about them.

"Fuck, they're perfect." My dick bucks in my trousers.

"Suck them, please." I nod and cup one in each hand, then take the left one in my mouth, sucking on it. She moans and gasps, rolling her hips on the bed. "Jack."

I can only grunt with my mouth full, but I indulge myself and move to the other and suck on it hard. She's going to make me come the way she's moaning. Her pussy must be juicing all over her thighs. I release one of her large mounds and slide down to her shorts, dipping my hands under the stretchy material, and run my hand between her legs.

"Fuck, you're so wet." I dip my finger into her slit. "Wow, you're going to come fast for me like you're supposed to."

"I'm going to come," she says, her fingers clinging onto my biceps, and she lets out a howling scream. I need to get unclothed because I want those claws digging into my skin, marking me up. She has no clue how much she has gotten under my skin, and I want the marks to prove it.

Fuck, it's beautiful the way she comes, but I catch her mouth because I don't want to scare John. When I pull back, I stare at my sexy woman, her face flushed, eyes glassy, and hair mussed.

"Take off your clothes. I need to be inside you. I want to fuck that tight little cunt until you scream my name," I command her while I tug off my tie. My clothes never came off so fast in my life, but it doesn't matter as I stare at the woman in bed looking like a queen fit for a king. "Are you sure you're a virgin? You look like a damn seductress sent to consume my soul."

"You're the one who consumed me, if my memory serves me correctly." Damn, that saucy mouth is going to get fucked soon. Not tonight, but soon she'll be on her knees, being punished with my big cock deep down her pretty, sassy, dirty mouth.

"Yes, I did, didn't I? Best meal I've ever had." I lick my lips and stalk toward the bed, stroking my length. A large bead of precum coats my tip, waiting for her sweet hole. Knowing her cunt is pure means she's more than likely unprotected, and the thought immediately gets me harder. Creating my heir fills my head and I stare at Nora, aching in every damn way.

"Open up. I want you to feed me."

"Come and eat." Nora parts her legs, and she's glistening all the way down from her sticky hole to her inner thighs.

"Fuck, baby girl. You're dripping for me." She nods and runs her hands all over her stomach, nerves getting the better of her. "Put those hands above your head. Don't hide anything from me. I want to see all of you, sweet, delicious Nora."

I glide my hands up her sinfully innocent legs that are about to be ruined for anyone else because they belong to me. The ruler of the MacNamara Empire. I run my mouth up her body, licking every inch of her, kissing my way until I reach her lips. "I love the way you taste, but I need to be in you before we're interrupted."

My fat tip rubs against her wet entrance and my pulse beats right there, throbbing to be in her. My muscles constrict as I press my hands down on the mattress. "Are you ready?"

"Yes, Jack." I push my way in, splitting her pussy lips open, and drive into her cunt hole. Inch by painfully slow inch, I claim her. She closes her eyes as I take her.

"Open your eyes and relax, my woman. You will look at me when I'm inside you." Her eyes flash open wide like I commanded.

"You're so big," she sighs, pressing her hands to my arms, and then pulls me down for a kiss.

"Fuck," I grunt, pulling out and pushing back in again. Her sweet pussy gushes around my length.

"You feel so damn good," I growl, working my hips. Ever since I saw her, I've been thinking about this moment. "Tell me how you're feeling."

"Full and good."

"I want you to feel wonderful and satisfied." I roll my hips and she moans, grinding hers upward as she clings to me. Pumping faster, I give in to her moans. She cries out, clawing my body as I suck on her supple tits.

"Fuck, I need to hear it. Come for me." Her walls flex tightly around my thick rod like a damn fitted glove. Even though she's soaked, she's still insanely tight.

"Jack," she screams. I wrap my hand around her hair and bring her mouth to mine, kissing her hard as I pump my seed into her womb and filling her up. I'm not done just yet, but I'm going to give her sore pussy a break. Getting up, I get a washcloth to soothe her.

We lay there for a bit, and then there's a knock on the door. "Shit, okay. It's probably my brothers."

"Hey, I have to get going," Connor says through the door. "John's sleeping, so you got some time."

"Thanks," I call out as I slip on my boxer briefs and walk to the door to speak with him for a minute. As he walks off, he says, "Take a shower; you smell like sex."

"Shut up and go home."

"I was already," he says, sticking out his tongue like he's a kid. I close the door and then turn back to see Nora getting dressed.

"Get back in bed and rest."

She tilts her head and sighs. "Thank you, but I have to take care of John soon."

I walk over to the bed and kneel with one knee on the mattress. Cupping her chin, I give her a deep, soul-searing kiss. "Leave that to me. Remember that you're not alone in this anymore," I say, giving her a kiss on her forehead.

"I'm going to shower, and then we'll eat some food because I'm starving and I'm sure you are too."

"Sounds good to me too." She sighs and falls back on the bed, looking exhausted and sated. I could totally get used to it.

CHAPTER FIFTEEN

NORA

JACK HAS TOO MUCH ON HIS PLATE, BUT THE first priority is to see his father this morning and let him know that he's found John. As much as I don't like it, we take John with us. Jack promises me that his father won't harm him, but I have my reservations. As much as Julia had lied to all of us, her love for John had been absolute, so there must have been some truth to her story.

So far, all three brothers seem to love him, although at this point, I can't tell if I'm wrong. Not one of them has been completely alone with him for an extended period of time, and it's not like they would try anything dumb that quickly again.

The exterior of his mansion isn't as nice as Jack's, but it's still insanely gorgeous and it's the closest to the entryway gate, which explains why it was easier to take John that day. I don't know any of the details, and of course I won't ask since it's none of my business. The less I know, the better, and that's the way it is when you're a part of a mafia family.

"Don't be so nervous. He's going to sense it and try to use it against you," Jack says.

"I'm not worried about me. Don't want him to hurt John." He stops me from getting out of the SUV with his hand on my wrist.

"Look at me." I do, and he stares into my eyes with such a fierce dominance that I'm almost lost in them. "He can't, and won't, do a damn thing to John. It would give him away, and that's not something he'd risk. My father's a lot of things, but being a fool isn't one of them. Do you trust me?"

It's not even something I think twice about. "Yes."

"Good. Now get your sexy butt out of the car, and let's greet the old bastard." I step out and walk around the vehicle to where Jack is helping John out of his car seat. Once he's on his feet, we walk to the front door and ring the doorbell, and a man quickly answers.

"Hello, Thomas. I'm here to see my father." Thomas's eyes drop to John, and he gasps.

"Yes, but don't say anything. I want to surprise him." He nods, and Jack takes my hand.

"He's in the dining room, sir. Please follow me," Thomas says. We step in behind him, and I hold on to John's hand while Jack takes the lead. I see the almost six-foot, paunchy elder MacNamara sitting at the head of the table.

"Jack, you've returned. What are you doing here without a call?" I don't like that tone.

"I thought you'd like a special surprise." Jack steps aside and lifts John up.

"My son, my baby boy, my Evelyn's baby," he says, jumping out of the chair with such exuberance that I'm surprised. "You're alive," he continues and nearly reaches out to touch him, but John turns inward, curling into Jack's chest.

"It's been a long time since you saw him, and the last time was traumatic."

"It most certainly was," he snarls. Then he looks over at me. "What the fuck is a Fieri doing with you?"

"Watch what you say about Nora. She's been taking care of John."

"You brought my son's kidnapper into my house?"

"She didn't kidnap him."

"No, she just held on to him without turning him over to the police or to us for the past year, and you expect me to believe that she's not involved?"

Oh, hell, no. I've hated this man from the moment we met and he told me that he had plans after I bore one of his sons an heir. He'd use me like one of his whores and pass me to his friends. I want to rip his head off, but for now I'm going to give him a piece of my mind.

Stepping up to his face, I puff up my chest and square my shoulders. "Excuse me. You have a lot of nerve. I just did what was best for John—something you seem to have neglected for the past five years of his life."

"Who the hell do you think you're talking to?" he questions, looking at me like I'm supposed to be intimidated. He has no idea the blade I hold over his head.

"I don't give a fuck who I'm talking to. So far, I've spoken to somebody who has always treated me extremely rudely. If it wasn't for me, John wouldn't be doing as well as he is or even be safe. So, you can think what you will, but I did what was best for him. And if you'd care to take notice, you'll see that he's grown in that past year."

"Yeah. All of a sudden he can do things that he couldn't do before because you were with him, and I'm supposed to believe that."

"It's true, Dad," Jack says.

"Maybe if you took the time to take your ego and put it away and focus on your child, then maybe you would have seen that he needed help. With all the money that you have, in a city with so many resources, he could have gotten the treatment he needed a long time ago. Children with autism flourish if they start young and get the assistance they need early on. He still has a chance to grow and embrace learning. If you're not so stubborn, he'll have a chance to have a semi-regular existence."

"I don't like your tone, young lady."

I scoff in his face, daring him because I've had enough of him. Suddenly all the fear I had at seventeen fades. The man I thought he was all those years ago seems to be worse than I imagined or exaggerated.

"Well, so far there's nothing I like about you."

He starts to raise his hand as if he was going to pop me in the face. "So help me God—if you put your hands on me, it will be the last motherfucking thing you do, old man. I don't take shit from men no matter how powerful they believe they are." I step back and glare at him, but it's the growl that comes from my side that causes him to step back.

Even though it appears Jack has no intention of acting, he moved John and had one hand in his suit jacket. "Chill out, Father. My fiancée is a little bit put out when you talk about John. She's worked very hard with him this past year, getting little to no sleep with him around."

"Fiancée? You're marrying her?" The bravado on his face fades.

"Yes. Is that a problem?"

"Of course it is a problem. We have no idea of her involvement."

"I know she's innocent." I love that he's sticking up for me with complete conviction and not letting this selfish prick change his mind. It hadn't occurred to me that it could be a possibility until now that we're standing in front of him, but these big brutes have a way of throwing their weight and power around.

"You can't be sure; it's just too convenient," he continues, glancing at me with a look of mistrust.

"Don't talk about convenience to me when you never wanted him around and then he disappeared." He storms off with me and John by the hand. "Come on. We're leaving."

We were in the vehicle within seconds. He wasn't wasting any time lingering at the house. Tension rolls off Jack like massive waves, and I'm afraid he's pissed at me. "I'm sorry I was so rude to your father."

"Don't worry about him. He's a blowhard that's trying to posture, but it's not going to work. By the way—we have a wedding to plan." I haven't forgotten about our arrangement. As much as I enjoy this passion between us, I remember that it's a temporary situation. I should ask about it, but I won't. There's too much going on to demand my freedom date. After all, I still have my home in Philly.

"Why isn't your dad fighting for John?"

"Because I already told him that if I found John again, he was mine and I wouldn't give him custody. Honestly, I think he prefers not having the responsibility of caring for him."

The second we got John down for a nap, the doorbell rings. Agnes goes to the entrance and opens the door. "Mr. MacNamara, what brings you here, sir?"

"I need to speak with my son."

"No, you don't," Jack snarls. "I'm pretty sure we just left your home, and there's nothing left to say."

"I want John back."

"That is tough shit because you weren't capable of taking care of him before."

"He's my son, not yours, and you don't have the right to him."

"Actually, when you were in the hospital, I was given power of attorney and I made sure to gain full custody of John. I'm the one who searched for him. Hell, you would have known that if you and your detective actually put any effort in your search."

"You're being difficult, Jack. I'll have my attorney look at the supposed custody documents."

"Go ahead. Now get out before you disturb John. Nora and I have a lot of wedding plans to make."

"When is this supposed wedding going to take place?"

"In two weeks."

"Does she know you refused to marry her before? She wasn't good enough because she's a Fieri. As you called them—trash." He's trying to needle me and put a wedge between Jack and me, but we've already discussed it, and I'm grateful that we had because it would have been a problem.

"Nice try with that, but we discussed the whole Fieri and MacNamara arranged marriage bit. Now—you heard my fiancé when he said to beat it."

"You better teach her to hold her tongue, Jack. She's going to be a problem."

"It's best if you leave."

"I'll be back with my lawyers." He turns around and leaves, slamming the door behind him.

"I'm sorry about him."

"Whatever." I walk over to the large picture window and watch to see if he drives away. He's gone, but the threat Julia mentioned still lingers in my mind. "Jack, did you ever find any of the other people involved?"

"No. It's strange; the only person I found was Joanne, which doesn't make any sense, and I'm not the one who found her."

"Who did?"

"Connor, but he got a tip from one of our guys who spotted her in town and then they tracked her down."

"That sounds pretty suspect. If she was running from you guys, why would she come back?" I already had a feeling in my heart, and it crushes me to the bone. She was leading them far away from John and me while sacrificing herself.

"Something is on your mind."

"Yes, it is. I don't know who else was involved in his kidnapping, but I do know that she was going to die of ALS, so she distracted you away from me."

"I wish things had worked out because I would have helped her with the medical treatment if she'd come to me in the first place."

"I don't know what her reasoning was. All I know is she said he wasn't safe with his family, and part of me still believes it."

"You don't believe any of my brothers would do anything, do you?" His mood darkens like I'm accusing his brothers of nefarious intent.

"No, I didn't say that."

"Good, because that's bullshit. They might not want kids right now, but they'd do anything to protect the family."

"Family includes your father?" I ask.

"Not anymore," he grunts.

"What does that mean?"

"Since our mother's death, we've had a strained relationship with him. We've all blamed him for her death."

"I'm sorry." I press my hand on his chest, feeling his heartbeat intensify as I hold it there. I want to tell him about what his father said, but the way he's looking at me, I forget all about the bastard because my future husband will protect me.

"Miss Fieri, you better be careful with the way you're touching me. I might have to show you what it does to me."

"Momma," John cries out.

"Hold that thought, handsome." I kiss his jaw and tend to his little brother.

CHAPTER SIXTEEN

JACK

"So how are the marriage plans moving along?" Connor asks after a blissful week at home. I've been so damn busy buried inside Nora that I nearly forgot about my other obligations. Connor and I headed to the docks where we received several shipments and oversaw some other matters before I could return to my beautiful fiancée and my little brother.

"Moving so damn slowly. I need to have her as my wife like yesterday." The frustration is damn near unbearable. Now that I have her in my life, I want her tied to me in every way. As we drive home, all I can think about is getting her in my arms even though I know Connor and I still have business to discuss.

"Well, don't let anyone stop you." My brothers have been extremely supportive about this. They're crazy about her especially after what she's done for John. Fuck, she should have been my wife years ago.

"Easy for you to say. I want to make it special for Nora. She deserves so much after everything that's happened." He nods.

"So how is Dad taking this whole situation between you two?" Connor asks, driving us back to the estate as fast as he can without breaking the law. He knows now more than ever that I hate taking too long to get back.

"He's asked about John, but that's it. You know he never gave a fuck about him, and it was just a show." The bastard tried to make a deal again, like he had anything to offer me. I'm not sure why he wants John back so badly. It's not as if he treated John as a father should treat a son that he claimed to love.

"Yeah, it was only because of Mom that he didn't send John away to a mental facility."

"It pisses me off. Nora told me that if he'd gotten more help sooner, he might be speaking full sentences." I shake my head, wanting to beat my father's ass. Hell, I want to kick my own ass for not taking the initiative, but our world was crumbling around us and losing our mother had been hard on us all. Still, I should have done more.

"Are you serious?" Connor snarls, slamming his hand on the steering wheel.

"Yes, so Dad might have kept John, but he didn't do a damn thing for him." We arrived at the reinforced gates and entered, monitoring the scene. I'm always looking for defects or ways for penetration after the last attack. There are always ways to get in, but I've added multiple layers of reinforcement.

"Well, at least you have Nora now who is a Godsend when it comes to John...and you." He nudges me with his elbow. We're almost halfway there and the run is overshadowed by storm clouds. Damn, I hope that doesn't frighten John. He didn't like storms before.

"She is great. Nora sent out the invites this morning, which will be interesting."

"What do you mean?" he asks as we pull up to my driveway. We dash up to my door. We don't get drenched because we're shielded by the portico.

"I told her to include her family." I say just as I open the front door and his mouth falls open.

"That's good. Do you think they're going to be pissed because there wasn't a deal this time around?" We walk to my office because I need to lock up my guns before I see John.

As we step inside I finally answer him, getting a glimpse of the shadow by the office door. "They can go fuck themselves. It's not like they had any hand in the relationship. If anything, they gave me damaged goods."

"Whoa, what the fuck, Jack?" Connor's eyes widened. I see Nora standing there behind me in the doorway.

"I'm only kidding," I insist, walking up to the love of my life and sliding my hands around Nora's waist, bringing my lips to hers, but she turns her face, and I catch her jaw.

"That's what I'd tell those assholes. I didn't get a mafia princess. I got a fucking fairy queen. I'm marrying the woman with a heart of gold."

"And a body that is…"

"Watch what you say," I snarl, tugging Nora tighter to my side. She giggles at my jealousy, but she has no fucking idea how insane I am when it comes to her.

"Going to give you kids," he teases, tossing me a smirk before downing a glass of whiskey.

"Anyway, before you rudely joked about our arranged marriage…I came to welcome you home and let you know that John was taking a nap. Now that that's done, I'll leave you two knuckleheads to discuss whatever thuggery you need to."

"Thuggery?" Connor asked, pressing his hand to his chest with a gasp.

"Yes, you heard me. Tell me I'm lying." She rolls her eyes.

I shrug because she's not wrong, but I'm not done with my sexy ass fiancée yet. "Well…at least give me another kiss before you go," I tell her.

"Fine," she huffs, and then turns her head upward with a pretty pout. I wrap my arms tightly around her round ass and kiss that smart mouth until she's moaning my name.

"Perfection," I whisper as our lips part. Her eyes widen and a smile lights her face.

"See you boys later."

"We're men," Connor shouts.

"Whatever." She waves us off and closes my office door. I smirk and shake my head, pouring myself a drink because my dick is so damn hard and I want to hunt her down and fill her up.

"So, any news on the fuckers who took John?" I ask my brother, needing a change in conversation.

"No, but Giles called and said that you weren't responding to his calls."

"Fuck. I meant to call him back, but I got a bit distracted last night and this morning."

"Be careful, Brother. Don't let pussy go to your head." He chuckles, pointing at my crotch.

"She's my wife," I snarl at him.

"Not yet."

"She may as well be."

"Yes, and we all love her, but you're the head of an empire and we have enemies who would love to take it over at all costs, including harming a beautiful little teacher with a heart of gold." Instantly my temper turns from joy to pure ire. If anyone dared to touch my Nora, I'd rip their heart out.

"You're right. Stay here while I make the call. I might need to handle some shit." He nods and sits down with his glass, and I dial Giles from my desk.

"Damn, you're a hard man to reach," Giles grumbles.

"Sorry, I'm not sure if you heard, but I just got engaged. What's going on, Giles?"

"I've got more info on that Julia Sanchez you asked about. She's the sister of Fernando Espi—" A door slams open on the other end of the line. "What the fuck are you doing here?" A shot rings out. Connor and I stare at each other.

"Giles, Giles!" I shout. Then the call is hung up. We both know damn well what happened. Someone gunned down my damn guy who gathered me intel. Was it because I asked him to pull info on Julia, or was it something he was tied to?

"Did he just say she's related to Fernando Espinosa?" Connor asks.

"He did. That motherfucker's involved somehow; I know it." He had to be involved and that made everything fit together. The wheels in my head start turning, contemplating all the ways I plan to torture Espinosa with my knives.

"Or maybe he just helped Julia escape. That could be the crux of it. He's a big pussy, but do you think he'd go to war with us just to get Joanne or Julia out from under our thumb? It doesn't make sense." My brother does have a point.

"Damn it. Is Giles still in Philly?" I asked.

"I thought so."

"I have to check it out. Can you stay here and watch over Nora and John? I'll ask Ian as well." They're the only ones

I trusted with my family. I sure as fuck wouldn't trust my father to the task.

"Of course, but do you think it's safe?"

"I'm not taking more than twenty-four hours. Hell, I might only be gone twelve because I refuse to leave them for so long." Shit, my chest aches to leave, but there's no way I'm leaving anything up to chance when it comes to them.

"That pussy got you good." If I didn't know better, I'd think he was jealous, but my brother loves her in a brotherly way and enjoys teasing me.

"Damn right. Excuse me, but I have to tell my bride-to-be to plan without me."

"Go ahead."

I fuck her twice before I board my private jet back to Philly. Leaving John was hard, but he was a good boy and clung to Nora.

The cops discovered Giles's body on the edge of town in the water, but I know damn well that wasn't where he was at. He more than likely had been in his hotel room, but I don't have access to it and I'm not going to leave my DNA anywhere near that shit, so Espinosa can tie shit to me.

I decide to go to Nora's old house and see if she needs anything while I plan my next move, but when I arrive my blood runs cold. This is the motherfucking crime scene. Giles had been inside Nora's home. Why?

Things are trashed, totaled, everything she owned ruined, but I can't fathom why. Thankfully, I'd decided to install cameras in her place before we left. They aren't hooked up to the internet, but they were activated via motion sensors. I have to pull the data, and then I can copy it.

I snatch the cameras and go straight to my rental and drive away, parking down the road two miles so whoever had been there doesn't see me. Turning on the video, I spot Giles. He's the one who comes in cursing.

"You fucking bitch. You picked that old fuck over me." He picks up a picture of Nora and John and then smashes it on the ground. "Damn it, I hoped you'd come back to me. His plan didn't work. I did all this for nothing. I hoped to get rid of that brat, but no, fucking bastard had other ideas." He picked up a bat and swung it around the room, smashing everything.

The bastard deserved to pay for what he did, and someone took him out. I wait for the footage to appear, and it does. I don't see who shoots him until he comes into the frame. It's fucking Espinosa. He picks up the picture frame and sighs. *"Fool. I should have killed the kid when I had the chance. Now, my sister's dead for nothing."*

Son of a bitch, it's all starting to make sense. Espinosa is involved in all of this. He killed Giles, had my brother kidnapped while killing a dozen of my men. I'm guessing Nora was a bonus to get us to turn on the Fieri family and start a war with them once she was found with John, but they underestimated my attraction to her and her willingness to protect him.

I drive straight to the airport and board my plane with all the evidence I need. Before we take off, I call my brothers. "How is my woman doing?"

"Good. She said she was taking a nap."

"And John, he's playing in the room with us. What information do you have for us? Please tell us you have something important to tell us." I tell them about Espinosa's involvement, but I don't understand Giles's comments and his interest in Nora.

"You should ask her."

"I will as soon as I get home." It's pissing me off that I don't have an answer, but there's nothing I can do about it.

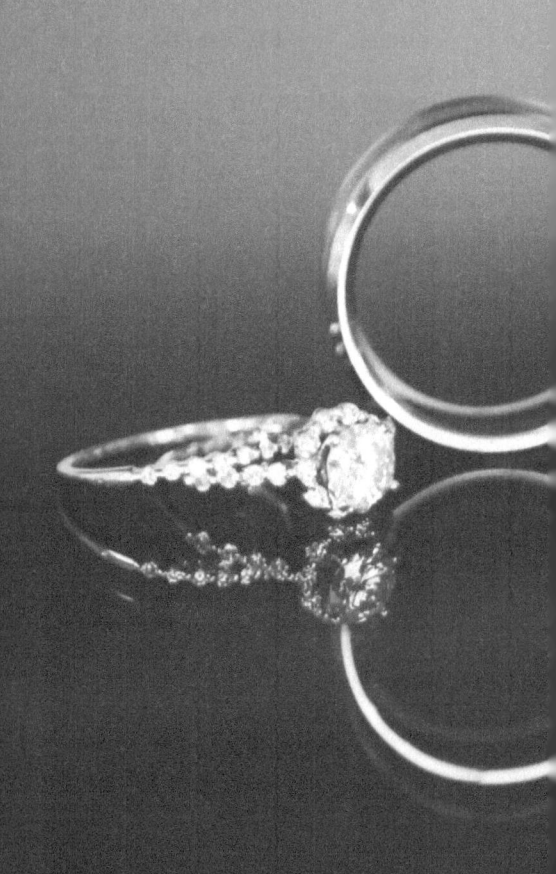

CHAPTER SEVENTEEN

NORA

I'd spent a couple of hours looking at wedding cakes and fell in love with these amazing cakes from this one girl on Instagram. They are fabulous, and I want one. She's so talented, and since Jack said I could have whatever I desired, this is the one thing I won't waver on. She's local, so I give her a call and she can meet on Friday.

Squealing, I freak and remember that the doors here are made of the best wood, but still I go to check on John and see how he's doing. He'd just gone down for a nap while I was doing my wedding planning, but when I entered his playroom, both brothers were sitting on the floor with him as he played. They look up and smile. Although they're siblings, they hardly look anything alike. You wouldn't know they're related if you weren't told.

"Hey, everything okay?" Connor asks me.

"Yep. Any news from Jack yet?"

"No, not yet, but he's probably still up in the air," Ian answers as he builds a plastic set of train tracks.

"How long are you guys sticking around?"

"Until he comes back," Connor answers, and Ian nods in agreement.

"Okay. I'm going to take a nap. Let me know if you need anything."

"Sure. You enjoy the rest while you can," Connor says.

I head back into the bedroom and lie on the bed, missing Jack. It's silly since he hasn't been gone long. Maybe it's because he went to Philly without me. It's technically my hometown. I could have gathered more of my things, seen Rebecca while he did his business. Stupid big jerk left me here, and I miss him. That's just the simple answer, and I hate myself for it. We've only known each other for a couple of days, and I've gotten used to him and his demanding and domineering ways.

I try to fall asleep when my phone rings. Assuming it's Jack, I answer without thinking. "Hello."

"Piccolina," my father's deceptively smooth voice answers. I pale and sit straight up.

"How did you get this number?" I question, my voice even tempered, almost annoyed. I stand up and walk straight to the guys. Without Jack here, I'm sure they'll want to hear this.

"A friend gave it to me. I hear congratulations are in order and you have finally agreed to the arrangement." The rat bastard.

As I enter the playroom, I wave my hand, and they come toward me. "I never agreed to it. Jack and I met by chance," I answer while the two giant MacNamara brothers gather around me.

I hold it out but don't put it on speaker so he doesn't get suspicious. They listen in closely. "Oh, my sweet girl. How did you make it all those years by yourself, and yet you are so naïve. That's what he wants you to believe."

"Why would I believe anything you have to say?" I challenged. Ian's hands flex.

"I didn't do anything any father in our organization wouldn't do. It's tradition, and even Jack will do it with your children. Do you think he suddenly just fell in love with you?" No, because we're not in love with each other. Lust, maybe. Goodness, we're definitely in lust, but he's almost forty and needs a wife. "I see I have my answer."

I roll my eyes. "What do you want?"

"You don't have to marry him. I have someone better for you." Connor purses his lips, holding back a scoff.

"I didn't fall for it the first time. What makes you think I'm going to fall for it a second time?"

"He's the one who killed your Julia, and he's the one who sent Jeremy to be your boyfriend and spy on you. Then our men just witnessed the killing."

"How do you know about Jeremy?"

"You think I stayed out of your life because I let you believe it. Your brother slipped up, and I found out where you were."

"I don't know what your end game is."

"I want their fortune. I want their surrender. You should be helping me, not them. So far, all these assholes have failed me. Espinosa had one shot after his sister failed me, and now if you disappoint me, I might have to kill your brother's new wife."

"Are you crazy?"

"The choice is yours. You have a day to think about it." He ends the call, and both brothers look at me.

"Don't even think about meeting with him. He's going to try holding you hostage, and no offense—my brother might enjoy screwing you, but it's only been a few days and he's not going to toss away his family empire for you," Connor says, and Ian nods.

"No shit, Sherlock." I slap him in the chest. "I don't even know what the old prick wants. He wants to kill me for defying him. Honestly, I think he wants revenge on everyone he can find. What I need to do is get a hold of my brother."

"He's going to be wise to it," Connor says, trying to warn me, but I know my brother and he and my father aren't tight.

I brush off his concerns. "Don't worry about it. I'll take care of it. Trust me when I say it will be easy."

Needing to handle some delicate matters, Ian leaves the house, promising to return in the morning.

Goodness, I wish Jack would call.

My phone rings just then. This time, I look and it's Jack. "Hey," I answered nervously.

"What's going on?" he asks with a strange, curious tone.

"What do you mean? I'm just picking out wedding stuff."

"So, you weren't on the phone with your father?"

"How the fuck do you know that? Are you spying on all my calls and messages?"

"No, but Shamus was about five feet away and heard part of the conversation and called me to give me a heads up on the situation. Whatever he told you was a lie."

"Trust me, almost everything he said, I didn't believe. He wanted to hurt me and separate us. I let your brothers listen in just in case."

"Smart woman."

"Do you know Jeremy, my ex?"

"Jeremy?" He draws out the name.

"Why did you say it like that? I mentioned him before."

"I know you did. Listen, there's something I need to talk to you about when I get home, but I promise you that it's not what you think." I don't like the sound of that, but like I said before, I believe him and I sure as fuck don't buy any of the bullshit my father said.

"Okay. I'll be here waiting for an explanation." I paced almost the entire first floor of the mansion waiting for him to return while Connor stared at me nervously. I gave John a bath, and now he's down for his nap.

"Will you tell me why you've done like a mini marathon in Jack's house for like three hours?"

"It's personal. I don't need you to stay, Connor. It's not like anyone is going to be stupid enough to break in here, and I know how to take care of John just fine."

"Well, I told Jack I would take care of you, and I will keep my word after what happened with John."

"Please. I'm just someone he met two days ago."

"Well, I was just being a dick to stop you from going. Jack has never given any woman his attention like this. Hell, I didn't think he'd ever get married unless it was arranged, and he set up the arrangement."

"Well, technically he did. This isn't love. This is an agreement for one year, two months and three days to pay for taking John."

"Damn, it's like that?"

"Yes, it is."

"It seems my fiancée needs a correction." Jack looks impeccable in his latest charcoal gray suit, white collared shirt, and matching gray tie.

"Okay, Brother. I'll just leave you to it. John's asleep, so hopefully you're good." He winks and walks out. I watch him walk away, and then my eyes are on the man who entered again.

"Nora, it seems we have a serious misunderstanding." He slowly yet deliberately stalks forward like a stealthy predator. I nearly fell back on my ass as I hit the back of the sofa. "I believe we've been here before."

"Not quite," I answered. He fists my throat, giving it a good squeeze.

"Better?" I nod.

"Now, listen, Miss Fieri. This isn't for one year, two months and three days. This is for the end of motherfucking time. You are mine. Mine. Do you understand me?" I nod again.

"Say it. Say you understand."

"I understand," I breathe out around his strong fist. My pussy throbs as I wear his five-finger necklace.

"Say you're mine forever."

"I'm yours forever."

"Good fucking girl." He rips off my shorts and stuffs his fingers into my heat, soaking them. "So damn wet for me. You like your necklace, don't you?"

"Yes, I do."

"Good, because so do I." He releases his cock from his pants and in one slick movement, he slams himself deep inside of me, lifting me onto the edge of the sofa. "Fuck, I missed you."

"Don't be gone so damn long next time," I demand. He fists my throat again and then licks my jaw.

"I can't promise that, but I promise to come home and fuck you until you can't walk," he grunts, pumping his hips forward until we're both covered in sweat and coming hard. I feel him unload all over my insides.

"You know I'm not on anything and we're not using any protection," I reminded him.

"Good. We're starting to add to the family," he grunts, he double pumps inside me a little harder, emphasizing his point.

"Are you serious? You don't mind?"

"Give me a minute and I'll show you again how serious I am, but first, we need to talk." I forgot about the entire reason I was upset—Jeremy.

He pulls out and tucks himself away before sliding my panties and shorts up, patting my panties against my mound. "I need to use the restroom and change."

"Fine. Let's take this upstairs. I'll check on John while you do that."

We meet in the bedroom twenty minutes later, and he's sitting on the bed in just a pair of boxer briefs and an undershirt. "What happened to you?" I ask.

"You were taking too long, so I decided to use one of the other showers." I blushed. Wanting to freshen up, I took a fast shower, but my mind started to wander, and wander. I guess I wandered too far off.

"Sorry."

"Don't be sorry. I plan on fucking you again," he growls.

"So tell me about Jeremy and you supposedly killing him."

"I don't know who this Jeremy asshole is, but I have a feeling I might. What I'm going to show you might be disturbing, and I'm only going to show you bits and pieces."

"Okay." He turns on a tablet, and it's my home and Jeremy comes onto the screen. "What's Jeremy doing in my house?" He starts ranting about me and marrying, kidnapping, and the works. I hear the call to someone and then the door opens. Jack puts the tablet to his chest for a minute, and then the gunshot goes off.

"You killed him?"

"No. I'm the one he's on the phone with. See, I didn't know that's the supposed Jeremy. That was my long-time associate, Giles. He and I go back about five years."

I gasp. "My dad said you sent him after me."

"Like I'd let another man taste these lips. Fuck. If I got a chance, I would have killed him myself. He set us up to find you and John. He knew I wasn't the kind to kill a woman, and he thought I would just leave you be." He caresses my cheek. "No way in hell did he think I'd fall for you, but I did. I fell fucking hard. I love you, Nora. I don't know when it happened, but you make me feel things I don't understand. Well, the lust I got, but there is so much more. Today, I understand completely. Being away from you was harder than anything I've ever done. The flight home was a nightmare thinking you might want to leave me over something I had nothing to do with."

"Jack, I love you too. I've been trying to figure this out. Yes, lust definitely contributed to it, but I feel safe when I'm with you and for a mobster, that's something I hadn't expected. Especially after having met your father before, I never wanted to be a part of the MacNamara family."

He lets out a deep chuckle with a nervous glint in his light eyes. "I can't say I blame you. Nora, marry me, not because I'm forcing you."

"Actually, I kind of like that idea." Something about Jack's domineering ways always sat well with me.

"Well, then, Nora, you will fucking marry me because I said so, and you know damn well I'll make you." He wraps his hand around my throat and pins me to the bed.

"You can't tell me what to do," I spit out through clenched teeth with his face inches from mine.

"The hell I can't."

"We'll see about that. I seem to recall something about being your daddy." He cocks his brow and grinds his fully covered cock against my aching center.

"Fuck. Why am I soaked?" I moan.

"Because you love being my bad girl who needs a lesson." He bites my ear, and I nearly come on the spot.

With great disappointment, he pulls back and stands, lifting me off the bed as well. We're both standing when he says, "But first, there's another piece of jewelry you're missing. I stopped at a jeweler while I was in Philly, but they didn't have what I wanted, so I did it this week and I picked it up on my way home today." Dropping down to one knee, Jack says, "Nora Fieri, you will marry me because I'll spank the shit out of you if you don't."

"Yeah, not a deterrent." I roll my eyes. He leans forward and bites my pussy. "Ouch, you asshole."

"Keep it up, and I'll fuck your little asshole." He wags his brows. I shiver, wondering if that's a threat or a promise. This man has brought out every filthy thought this inexperienced woman has had.

"Fine. I guess I'll marry you." He chuckles and slides a huge rock on my finger. My mouth falls open. "Oh my goodness. This is massive."

"Only the best for the queen of the MacNamara Empire." He stands up and growls, "Where were we?"

My eyes widen and I let out a giggle before I find myself planted back on the bed and in for an intense fucking reunion.

CHAPTER EIGHTEEN

JACK

"Bend over and keep those legs open for me. I'm going to fuck you so damn good today. You've made me hard and angry. What would possess you to date some piece of shit like that? You should know better."

"He wasn't ugly," she teases, popping her hips back so her ass jiggles in front of me.

A growl rips through my chest like a beast. Giles had been a friend of mine until he betrayed me, and then knowing he planned on fucking my woman, I wish I'd been the one who killed him. He'd known where my brother was, he'd helped Espinosa and inserted himself in my woman's life, and only alerted me to my brother because he finally wanted to get my brother out of her life so he could get back into it.

I hated him. Unfortunately, the bastard wasn't here for me to take my frustration out on, so I'll get to give her what she asked for. "I promised you a spanking, and it's time I delivered." My hand comes down on her soft, creamy white ass.

———

I COULDN'T BELIEVE WHAT MY FATHER SAID TO her; actually I could, but I couldn't believe that she waited so long to tell me. When she finally confessed it to me I wanted to go over to his house and rip his head off, but she begged me to let it go. He was just trying to scare her back then or so she claims, but I call bullshit because I wouldn't put anything past that asshole.

Still he'd never get that far. I'll castrate that fucker if he even considered it. I wasn't in the right frame of mind to deal with the baker or any other wedding planner shit right now because I had to have a talk with my men.

I make a call to my brother, needing to appease my bride before the big day. It's a silly request, but for her I'd do anything and she deserves to have something special for her wedding after everything she's been through.

"Connor, I know you're busy, but can you do me a favor and go to the bakery for me?"

"What? I'm kind of busy. I've been dealing with the shit you've been letting slide over the past three weeks."

"I'm sorry, but something has come up and Nora will be upset if I ruin the baker appointment. Apparently, she's super famous, and she made this fabulous cake that caught Nora's eye while I left her trapped in the house."

"Is she still pissed about you going out of town?" he asks with a chuckle. The bastard took great pleasure out of my troubles with Nora. I think he's rooting for Nora to give me hell, but he's lost this battle.

"No, I made it up to her several times."

"Lucky fucker," he grumbles.

"Damn right, I am. I want to have a word or two with her family today." I need to know what deal they had in place with my father.

"You sure you don't want backup?" His sense of foreboding is well deserved because those assholes can't be trusted and they aren't worth my time, but this isn't for me.

"I'm taking Ian with me for this one."

"That's what I was going to suggest. There's no damn way I'm in the mood for it. I'm already tired."

"Too much partying?" He's been busy with helping me with John and running the empire, including the nightclub. He has no time for shit, not even to walk his dog who is probably chewing up his Italian loafers.

"No, I had a run-in with that dickhead governor," he grunts.

"And you didn't tell me?"

"You're in your own happy little world and have enough on your plate. Besides, I'm a big man. Dad hates that prick and keeps picking fights with him, so his people pulled a raid on the club last night and had it shut down for no reason. I was able to get it taken care of, but it cost us about ten grand. I'm going to sue them, but it will probably cost as much as we lost in just the legal fees alone."

"That prick knows what he's doing. We need to have a talk with Dad again and tell him to quit it with the asshole. The war has to end because it serves no purpose. Two old bastards going head-to-head, and the only ones paying for it are us."

"So damn true. Send me the address, and I'll take care of it."

"I owe you one, Connor."

"That you do, but I'm not doing it for you. I'm doing it for my favorite sister-in-law. I owe her," he says, and that makes me wonder what they aren't telling me.

"Why do you owe her?" I asked, wanting the details.

"You're not an asshole anymore," he laughs.

"Fuck off."

"Maybe I don't owe her." I could kick him in the balls. Sometimes I miss beating my brother's ass. When we were younger, we would spar and wrestle while training and I'd always kick Connor's ass even if he tried to cheat. Fighting with Ian was a little rougher because he was always angry, and that temper drove him to go wild. He was the enforcer for a reason.

"Just do it for us," I snarl.

He chuckles and ends the call, so I pull up the information Nora sent me on the wedding cake designer and forward it to him.

Now I can finish what I planned, and Nora can meet with the instructors that will see John on a regular basis at the house. As much as she can do, it would be better if she had help. I refuse to leave him in her care alone. That's why she was drowning before. I've vetted them before I allowed them to come to my home and there is extra security, but each of the women come from a professional background with no ties to our worlds.

Finally, I'm off to deal with these fuckheads. With several of my men, I entered my special warehouse on the Northside with the two Fieri men. "Mr. Fieri, thank you for seeing me. I heard you spoke with my fiancée two nights ago."

"Yes, and she wasn't very agreeable." The audacity of the old fuck pisses me off. I could snap his neck right now. He has no idea what I'd do for my sweet Nora. Every enemy she has is now mine. If I could have destroyed Giles, I would have. It still pisses me off that I missed it. At least I got to him in the end. It destroyed him to know I was fucking her.

"Well, what would you expect since you treated her as a commodity and not the precious child she is?" I reminded the bastard that was my special guest.

"She's a daughter, and that's what she's good for," he scoffs, tugging on his ropes. There's no way he's going to get out of them. Shamus is an expert at tying them.

I fist his hair and hold a blade to his skinny, pencil-neck throat. "Watch your tongue before I cut it out of your mouth." I hated this man and every word he uttered was a waste of my time that took me away from Nora. She fled her life because of him and had to start all over in a whole new state just to avoid his wrath.

"Why am I here? I didn't do anything against my sister?" Massimo Fieri says.

I smile at him which immediately unnerves the elder Fieri. "No, you didn't, but I want to broker a deal. I'll let this fucker live, if you deal with Espinosa. I want him out of our lives for good." Espinosa is a problem, and I don't have time to devote to hunting him down personally without leaving my family behind, but I also can't risk him living and running around ready to strike again.

"It's not that easy. He's a piece of shit, but he's got the cops on his side and I don't know who else is helping. He's slimy and slips through everything I've tried to get him on," Massimo says.

I know. Fucking hell, don't I understand that. "I know. I should have put a bullet in him when I had a chance."

"You should have because he's going to come after you and my sister. Now I'm going to have to hunt him down." Enrico Fieri is staring at us with greedy ears, listening too much, but that didn't matter because he wasn't leaving this building with a pulse.

"He already sent that fucking boyfriend after her. The one you knew about."

"I didn't know she had a boyfriend. I was just trying to deter you," Massimo says. "The last time I spoke to my sister, she'd just started her first year of teaching and I let her be."

"Well, Daddy here said he found her because you gave him the details."

He shakes his head and lets out a harsh scoff. "I wouldn't give him a thing on her."

That's when Enrico gets bold. "Come on. It's not that hard to dig into your personal things when you were busy with your whore." Now the old man fucked up and I laugh.

"Don't you dare talk about her like that." He jumps out of his chair, not really tied down. He grips the rope and wraps it around his father's throat, choking him. Leaning down, he snarls, "What did you do to my sister? What did you threaten to do to my woman? Did you think she wouldn't alert me?"

I thought my father was a piece of shit, but it seems the Fieri patriarch took the cake. He betrayed both his children. My father is just a neglectful asshole who got my mother pregnant when she was way too old to be having babies.

Enrico's head slumps forward and Massimo stands, straightening his suit. "Sorry, I lost control."

"No, I'm sure you've had years of pent-up rage waiting for that shit. It was happening one way or another. He crossed the line with Nora, so if you didn't, I was ending that fucker," I say.

Fieri's men and mine work together to deal with his father's lifeless corpse, and then Massimo Fieri asks, "Was that a true invite to the wedding?"

Smiling, I say, "Yes. Nora wants you there."

"I wouldn't miss it for the world." The look of joy on his face reminds me that they're siblings and I'm glad that I didn't have to kill him. Nora will be so happy that he'll be in her life. We shake hands and then we part ways. I head back, anxious to see my woman.

I'm almost home when I get a call from Connor. "It was a motherfucking setup." Son of a bitch. I turn the SUV around and plug in the address for the bakery. Someone's a dead motherfucker.

"I'm on my way."

EPILOGUE

NORA

DECEMBER 2014

There's a light, fast knock on the door. "Come in." It opens, and I'm surprised to see who is there. He steps inside and closes it.

Massimo stares at me from across the room. "You look beautiful," he says.

"Thank you," I say, looking at him from the mirror. He's as handsome as ever in his tuxedo. In fact, I think he's grown up a little more now that he's not under my father's thumb anymore.

Although, I'm not sure what happened to my father, other than he was supposedly killed by Fernando Espinosa. The men are still looking for him, but they've had no luck since he's been on the run for weeks now. We even had to push our wedding back due to the attack on Connor and the trouble that caused.

He reaches out and takes my hands in his, extending them to the sides and staring at my gown while giving my hands a gentle squeeze. "You are radiant, Nora. An absolute gem. I'm glad you allowed me to be here today. I want you to know that I had nothing to do with Father's attempt to marry you off all those years ago, and I hope you believe that."

I nod. "You know, Massimo, you were the only one I never blamed in all of this. It's not like you had much of a choice either. He wanted you to marry someone else too."

"Thanks." He pulls me in for a hug. "I missed you so much, Nora."

"Would you do me a favor?"

"Anything?"

"Walk me down the aisle." My brother's face brightens, and a smile breaks out across his handsome mug.

"I would love nothing more." He hugs me again. "When Jack threatened me that he was marrying you and there was nothing I could do to stop it, I was so fucking afraid for you, but now I see that you're so happy. It does my heart a world of good." He kisses my cheek and says, "He better be good to you because I'll go to war for you."

The music begins, and my brother extends his arm. Today is going to be perfect now.

EPILOGUE

JACK

May 2025

"Caleb, what did you do?" I ask the second I enter the conference room in the private school my wife teaches at and that our oldest attends. The police haven't arrived yet because they have more important matters to attend to and didn't deem this one important. Or rather, they know better than to try and arrest my ten-year-old son.

"Father, they earned it. They're lucky that's all they got." A cough comes from behind me, immediately annoying the shit out of me. I turn around to see an impeccably dressed older man that I've seen on occasion on camera checking out my wife. He and I have needed to have a talk in private more than once, but I let it go because she's asked me to. Today, I'm not feeling so generous.

"Quiet right now, Caleb. I want to speak to the principal, since he seems to not be able to control his bladder." The man is doing a pee dance, moving his legs back and forth, rocking himself like he's anxious to speak with me or like a child needing to use the bathroom. He blanches at my perfectly aimed insult.

He sputters before using his voice. "Excuse me, sir. Your son assaulted two boys in class today. He broke their noses and gave them two black eyes."

"Where are the parents of the other kids?" This incident had just occurred, and I rushed here from an important meeting. Hell, my wife is still teaching in her class. Why wasn't she called into the meeting before the police were called?

"They had to take the kids to the hospital."

"Very well. I'll speak with them privately."

"I don't believe that will be necessary."

"Well, I do."

I don't care for his accusatory tone one bit. There is a strange way he's phrasing it. The cops called me forty-five minutes ago, so Nora should have already contacted me, but according to the camera in her classroom, she hasn't left the room and no one has entered. In our eleven years together, we've had our ups and downs, but one thing hasn't changed—I'm proud of her skills as a mother and as a special education teacher, so when she asked to go back and do it, I jumped right on board. She's been working at this school for three years now, and I can't stand the number of motherfuckers that eye fuck my wife. Still, I understand she's gorgeous, so it's bound to happen.

Only a few didn't take "no" or "I'm married" for an answer, and I had to step in to set the record straight. Now, this fuck knew she was married so he never outright hit on her, but I saw the camera feeds. I watched how he stared at Nora like a lovesick fucking puppy, eyeing her to the point of a dangerous fetish. I want to rip his head off, but I maintain my composure.

"Like my son said, they earned it, so explain to me what happened."

"I'm not sure. The boys said he just attacked them in class unprovoked."

"That's a lie," Caleb shouts.

"Son, we don't raise our voices like that. Now, do tell me what really happened."

"You're not going to like it."

"Were they speaking inappropriately about your mother?" He shakes his head, and the bastard who thinks he's won releases a smug puff of air. "Watch that," I warn him, and he stiffens.

"Son, just tell us."

"They insulted John. They called him stupid and weird." My little scrapper has tears in his eyes, and I can't blame him for it. My kiddos love their uncle as much as their momma and I do. My fists clench so damn hard on the wooden chair in front of me that it cracks.

"Are you mad at me?"

I cup his face and pull him in for a hug. "Of course not. Never, Son. You did the right thing, and I'm sure they learned their lesson."

"Mr. MacNamara, that's not how we teach lessons on name-calling here."

A growl rips from my body, and I release my son before turning my rage on the damn principal. Keeping my calm, I focus on him. "Apparently you don't even acknowledge anything happened, so you don't teach anything. It's twenty-twenty-five; autism has long been discussed, understood, and worked on. The stigma isn't there like it was before. You and your staff should be well aware of it. This is a fucking expensive private school."

"Darling, what are you doing here?"

"Nora, didn't you hear? Our son was nearly arrested for assault today in school for beating up two classmates."

"What?" Her tiger eyes turn completely round.

"Yes. Your dear principal didn't call you in here yet. I got a call from the police department first."

"Oh, my goodness. Are you okay, Caleb?" He nods. She bends down and hugs our baby before standing up and glaring at the principal. "How dare you call the police on my son?"

I grab her and hold her back before she can attack the man. "Sweetheart, you're carrying my baby, and remember —I don't like another man's hands on you in any way."

"You're right. I should have known this was coming. Jack, the police aren't coming for my baby, are they?" she asks, looking up at me with pleading eyes. I kiss her lips softly.

"Love, not a damn chance in hell. Do me a favor and take our son to get his things. I'm taking him home. I understand if you need to stay with the kids for the day. Shamus will stay by your side until the end of the day."

"Okay." She kisses me again and then gives the principal a scathing look before taking our son's hand. The second that the door closes behind them, my attention returns to the good principal who doesn't have the common sense to stop staring at my wife through the window in the door. "She looks good?"

"Yeah. What? I mean no. I mean…" he stammers.

"Stop right fucking there."

"I know what you're fucking playing at. I know what you were planning to do. See, my wife would do anything for her family, but what you forget is that this here…" I wave my wedding ring in his face "…makes me a part of her family. Did you think you'd get the cops here, tell her that they'd take her son to jail and that if she didn't give you what you want, they'd toss him in jail?"

He gasps as if I figured out his stupid plan. I knew the second my wife wasn't in the office that he wasn't planning on arresting my son. He wanted to force my wife to behave and submit. "No one but me makes my wife behave and submit. No one."

"I wasn't…" I grip him around the throat, squeezing tightly. The stench of piss fills the air quickly. "So, you did have to go."

"Please don't kill me."

"I'll consider it if you tell me the truth. What were your plans?"

"I wanted her to have sex with me."

"You shouldn't have told me that."

"You said if I told you the truth—"

"I'd consider letting you live. My wife is going to finish out the school year and so are you. You're going to act like nothing happened, and if I catch you even glancing in my wife's direction, I'll gouge out your eyes with an unsharpened pencil and enjoy it. Understand?"

He nods and I release the fuck, letting him fall in his own piss. "Stay away from my family."

I leave the office and see my son waiting for me with his things. "Let's go get some ice cream."

"Can we pick up John?"

"Absolutely." I call his school and tell them I'm coming to get him. Once I arrive, he's in the office with a smile, a smile that my wife fostered. "Jack, Caleb."

"John, we're getting ice cream. Do you want to come with us?"

"Cookies and cream?"

"If you want." He starts rocking back and forth, clapping his hands, and I wrap my arm around his shoulder. "Come on, buddy."

"How was school?"

"No school." He's still having a difficult time, but we're trying to branch out from the house and give him a little more freedom. He'll never get the life our other children will, but we'll do everything we can to make him happy. Caleb is one hell of a buddy to his uncle.

"I don't like it either, Uncle John." I take John's book bag and sign him out.

"Mr. MacNamara, I just want to let you know he's improving. Slowly, but we're seeing progress in his test scores. I wanted to give this to you." She hands me a math test, and I see his grade. He scored an eight out of ten. Tears fill my eyes. I just threatened to murder a man, but I'm about to cry like a little bitch because my brother can do basic math at almost seventeen years old. "Thank you. My wife will be so thrilled."

"Congratulations." We have been working so hard with him over the years, but unfortunately some things won't stick. Nora works with teams, and we have our home full of people to teach John, but his mental growth has leveled out. A part of me wonders if he suffered from my father's physical abuse or if it's because he's lower functioning on the autism spectrum from a level three to now more of a level two. I love my brother, so it doesn't matter. I'm just happy to see him smile. These moments bring me peace.

We get home just as my wife and our two other children arrive at the house, and she's scowling at me. "What's wrong, my love?"

"Momma Nora," John shouts, hugging her a little too aggressively. I have to remind him to be gentle all the time since he's grown to be nearly as tall as me.

"Too hard, John."

"Sorry. We had ice cream."

"What did I say about the secret," I whisper to him.

"Oh…" He giggles.

"Go get cleaned up while I talk to Jack," she tells him. "Caleb, give me a hug too." He smiles and gives her a hug. He runs off, and I know I'm all alone to face her wrath.

"Did you pull John out of school again?"

"What? It's not a big deal."

"It is, if he's going to start expecting you to pull him out all the time. How many times has it been this year?"

"Only six times."

"Why does it feel like more?"

"Because you're worried about him and how he reacts to everything. Nora, you've been a wonderful mother to him and our babies too."

"I'm just worried about him. He hates school as it is, and it's so much harder there."

"Well, then let me show you this." I pull out the math test and show it to her.

"Oh, my goodness." She bawls like a baby, tears falling down her reddened cheeks. "This is so great. I can't believe it."

"Me either. He's growing." I wrap my arms around her and embrace the love of my life. "I love you, Nora. I couldn't have done this without you. John's safety and growth were all your doing." We slowly closed our lips, moving in for a deep, meaningful kiss. Our love will forever be on display and so damn present. I'll never get enough of this woman.

"Thank you, but you never gave up on him and that makes all the difference. I love you, Mr. MacNamara."

"You're so sexy," I growl.

"Don't think I forgot about your conversation with the principal. They said he left early for the day. Will he be returning?"

"For a short while, and then maybe he'll have an accident."

"Why? Because he was going to arrest our son?"

"No, because he wanted what was mine and planned on using our son to get it."

"Gut the fucker. I'd never."

"I know you wouldn't, and he's a fool to think you'd even consider it. Don't think about that pussy anymore. He's not worth your time, so let's go upstairs and let the cook finish dinner while you and I have a private conversation about how you belong only to me."

"Children, behave. Daddy and I need to discuss what happened today at school. Please be good. Dinner should be ready soon."

"Okay, Mommy." Our babies are well behaved. The two younger ones are playing with their Legos, and Caleb and John are playing with toy cars on a large floor mat.

Our talk goes longer than expected as my wife takes pleasure in submitting to me, even if she refuses to behave. "Baby, you're going to need to wear a scarf to dinner tonight. That neck is a little red."

"Fuck, Jack," she complains, running over to the mirror. "Not again."

"You asked for it. Maybe you'll learn to behave."

"Never." She cups my cock. I grab her around the throat.

"Wife, you know we don't have time for another fucking. You're lucky we only have sons. I'd hate to have a little princess seeing me walk around sporting this fucker because you're a bad girl."

"I'm sorry." She drops to her knees in front of me, freeing my aching cock from my charcoal gray slacks. "I'll take care of it."

"Now you want to behave. Good. I'm going to be quick, and you're going to take this dick hard and fast. I'm going to fuck that gorgeous mouth and remind you that you're mine. Only I get to stuff it, own it while I cuff your sexy throat, cutting off your breath."

"Yes, Jack," she moans, breathy already.

"Open," I commanded. The way she does makes me want to come in her pretty mouth so fast. I slide my dick past her plump red lips. "Love the lipstick, baby." She smiles and then takes me inch by inch, gagging as I push deeper into her throat. After all these years, I know she can take me all the way. Fuck, it's a little treat I learned and loved. "Suck."

With hollowed-out cheeks, she sucks out my soul until I'm howling with one fist wrapped around her hair and my hand holding her still, gripping her throat. "Let me fuck that mouth." She nods, and then I start taking total control, owning my wife's slender column while she owns my orgasm. Each thrust that ravages her face nearly breaks my will, and I'm on the verge of nutting when I hear her fingers teasing her sopping wet cunt.

"Damn it, baby." I pull out, my dick dark and veiny, ready to burst. "On all fours."

She drops onto her hands and knees on the plush carpet. Kneeling behind her, I press my fingers into her soaked entrance and find my wife more than ready. With one push of my cock, I impale Nora, bottoming out in her.

"Fuck, you're so deep."

"That's right. Who do you belong to?"

"I belong to you, Jack."

"That's right. Who loves you and would give you anything in the world?"

"You," she pants, pumping her ass back. I lean over her slender frame and cup her tits, rubbing them, and she gasps in pain.

"Whoa, baby. They're a bit sensitive. I lose control and forget how tender they can be."

"Don't be. I love your touch, even when it's rough," she moans, giving me an extra squeeze around my hard cock.

"Thank you, my love." With a final thrust, I grunt my load into her, coming deep inside.

"Wow, that was intense."

"Yes, it was. So, same time tomorrow?"

"Maybe after the kids are in bed." She giggles.

"Fine," I tease.

When we finally make it down, the kids have finished up their homework and they're getting ready for dinner. Nora loves having help for moments like these. The rest of the evening is spent with our kids, and then they're off to bed. Life couldn't be any better.

THE NEXT MORNING, NORA GETS A PHONE CALL, and her mouth falls open. "What's wrong?" I asked my gorgeous but dismayed-looking wife.

She plopped down on our bed. "School's been canceled today. Principal Lassiter is dead."

"What?" I questioned. "I didn't order it." I threw my hands up.

"He died in a drunk driving accident last night. Apparently, he got pretty wasted and drove himself out of town. His vehicle was packed, and he crashed on the expressway."

"It looks like the trash took itself out." I'm happy that I didn't have to deliver my own justice to that fucker because I sure as fuck had ever intention of dealing with the principal in time.

"I couldn't agree more." She runs her hands over her face and then through her hair. "Let's keep all the kids home."

My mouth drops open at her suggestion. "Ha—now who is the one giving John the wrong expectations?"

"Don't start with me. I'll give you the wrong expectations, mister." She flashes me her breasts and then takes off running while giggling, but that's where she's wrong. I don't expect anything but enjoying the rest of my life with my beautiful family, starting with some pancakes.

THE END

ABOUT THE AUTHOR

Find out more about Carina Blake:
Website: www.carinablake.com
Facebook: www.facebook.com/AuthorCarinaBlake
Instagram: www.facebook.com/AuthorCarinaBlake
Tiktok: www.tiktok.com/@carinablake
Bookbub: www.bookbub.com/profile/carina-blake

ALSO BY CARINA BLAKE